"You must be joking.

Her words came out clipped, but it felt like they were spoken through mud.

Gregory placed both palms on the counter. "I assure you, I'm not."

Vanessa's throat tightened almost painfully, and she could have drowned in the confident intensity of his hazel eyes.

"And I can assure *you* that I'm not interested."

Gregory took a step back. "Really? I'm surprised. Your father told me that flowers aren't your only talent. He said you also have a knack for public relations, and that you've been especially successful helping politicians in a crisis."

Vanessa's stomach burned with resentment. Her father had no business talking to the mayor about her, but she'd deal with him later.

In Gregory's voice, she heard no trace of disdain, and that was good. There were only two people who knew the sordid details of her stint in political public relations, and that was the way it would remain. She was a pro at hiding the secrets of powerful and successful men, and even better at hiding her own.

Vanessa tilted her head. "Oh, so you're admitting your reelection campaign is in trouble?"

"Not trouble," he insisted, lifting one finger. "Just a bit of a rough spot."

She broached a wry smile. "I'd say you're at the top of a raging waterfall about to crash to the rocks below."

Gregory leaned in closer. "I like to live dangerously," he murmured in a low voice.

Dear Reader,

Winning Her Love is the first book of my Bay Point Confessions series, set in a fictional small California town.

Meet Mayor Gregory Langston. He must win another term in order to see his redevelopment plan for the city come to life.

And Vanessa Hamilton. She's got a passion for flowers and the century-old Bay Point carousel. She agrees to help Gregory gain support from the locals when he promises not to demolish the carousel—if she can find a way to save it.

There's something about a carousel that is magical. Unexplainable. Puts a smile on your face. Sometimes it's so hard to choose the perfect horse to ride. They're all so beautiful and so tempting. The same can be said of falling in love, right?

I hope you enjoy reading this book and that you'll stay tuned for others in the series.

Be blessed,

Harmony

Winning
Her
Love

Harmony Evans

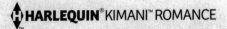
HARLEQUIN® KIMANI™ ROMANCE

Recycling programs
for this product may
not exist in your area.

ISBN-13: 978-0-373-86402-7

Winning Her Love

HARLEQUIN®

Printed in U.S.A.

™ www.Harlequin.com

Harmony Evans received the 2013 Romance Slam Jam Emma Award for Debut Author of the Year. Her first book, *Lesson in Romance*, garnered two RT Reviewers' Choice Award nominations in 2012. *Winning Her Love* is her fifth book for Harlequin Kimani Romance. She currently resides in New York City. Connect with Harmony on Facebook, Twitter or at harmonyevans.com.

Books by Harmony Evans

Harlequin Kimani Romance

Lesson in Romance
Stealing Kisses
Loving Laney
When Morning Comes
Winning Her Love

Visit the Author Profile page at
Harlequin.com for more titles.

To my daughter, Angelina. Meow! I miss you.

Chapter 1

Gregory Langston jutted his fists knuckles-down against the windowsill and stared outside. The sun was at the halfway point in the sky, hanging around the corner of dusk. It would be dark soon. If he was going to see Vanessa, he'd better go quickly, before she closed the shop for the evening.

He squinted involuntarily at the orange-red orb blazing away in the distance. The California sun was gloriously dangerous yet absolutely necessary to his survival, just like the risk he was about to take.

"I have to win," he muttered fiercely under his breath.

Although he was only thirty years old, Gregory had achieved more than many men had in a lifetime. At age twenty-six, he became the youngest and the first African-American mayor in Bay Point, California. He'd won the esteemed position in a landslide victory four years earlier, an accomplishment of which he was extremely proud.

Now he was up for reelection. But this time victory would not come easily. His only rival in the mayoral race was making his campaign a living hell.

Jacob Billingsly "the Third and only," as the man liked to put it, had lived in Bay Point for only a few years, yet acted as if he'd resided there his entire life. When Jacob had announced his plan to run for mayor, no one had been more shocked than Gregory, who had taken the young upstart under his wing and given him a paid internship as a mayoral clerk for two summers. When Jacob had graduated with an MBA from Stanford University, Gregory had given him a glowing reference for a potential employer in New York City. He'd even driven Jacob to the airport on what was supposed to be his last day in Bay Point.

As it turned out, Jacob never left, and now it seemed he spent most of his time spreading rumors and lies about Gregory and his plans for Bay Point.

The knot in his stomach tightened and Gregory closed his eyes, bracing for the pain, which was happening all too often lately.

Although Gregory would never admit it to anyone, he was scared he was going to lose his reelection bid. The thought that he might have made a mistake by choosing a career in politics kept him up night after night. Maybe he should have continued working in his father's law firm instead of trying to fix the town that he loved more than anything.

His eyes drifted from the horizon to the storefronts and streets beneath his fourth-floor office. The traditional grid-like pattern appealed to his strong sense of order.

In its heyday, Bay Point was a hideaway for California's rich and famous, particularly actors and actresses from Los Angeles who sought a temporary escape from a lifestyle that often demanded too much. The whimsical shops and cheery restaurants amid the sultry ocean breeze were a balm to their weary souls. The stars still journeyed to the town from time to time, but not enough to stir headlines or the attention of entertainment bloggers.

But now Bay Point, whose population was about ten thousand individuals of all races and ethnicities, was in serious trouble. Located on the beautiful Pacific coast between San Francisco and the Oregon border, the once-vibrant beach town had fallen on hard times in recent years. Many longtime residents had moved due to the recession and high unemployment rate. Newcomers were few and far between.

Gregory knew he needed to bring additional revenue into the area to attract new residents or, at the very least, tourists. And he needed to give the people already there a reason to stay. Redeveloping Bay Point's quaint but aging downtown was the only way to begin to breathe new life into a town that was in danger of dying.

Gregory grimaced and stuck two fingers of his left hand inside his blue oxford shirt, attempting to massage away the painful knot beneath his rock-hard abdomen. The residents of Bay Point trusted Gregory to bring the town back to the prosperity it had once known. They had elected him into office, believing that he could enact lasting change. He couldn't let them down, but the truth was, he was afraid he already had.

This morning he'd unveiled his plans to redevelop downtown Bay Point in the *Bay Point Courier.* The three-year project, which took about that much time to actually scope and plan, would bring much-needed jobs, new retail and new housing to the area.

He'd tried to keep many of the details under wraps as the plan was being solidified so that residents wouldn't be alarmed. But Bay Point was a small town, and some folks just couldn't keep their mouths shut. Now that all the details were in print, many weren't happy.

To make way for the construction of a brand-new municipal complex, the project also included the demolition of the Bay Point Carousel. To Gregory's surprise, this seemed to elicit the most unfavorable responses among his constituents. The phone had rung off the hook all day, and his inbox was flooded with angry emails.

"Not good," he muttered.

He peered at the hundred-year-old carousel, located in the center of downtown, and wondered why it held such an appeal to everyone. He understood the structure's historical significance. But it was a drain on the city's budget, and it was almost always broken-down. It had to go.

Gregory withdrew his fingers from his shirt and cranked open the casement window. He needed the favor of Bay Point residents, but more important, he needed their votes in order to be elected to a second term as mayor. Somehow he had to get them back on his side. He had to make them see the beauty of his vision for the city. Tearing down the carousel would be a good thing. A new beginning.

He ran his hand down his face. Two knocks and a tap on the door jolted him from his thoughts.

"Come in," he grunted.

The door opened. "Mayor Langston, is it all right if I leave for the day? My son has his first soccer practice tonight and—"

Mariella Vency, his executive assistant, was a single mother whose teenage son had a tendency to get into trouble. He knew that she was trying to encourage better behavior through participation in organized sports. They'd recently moved to Bay Point from Los Angeles, and the boy had few friends.

She paused and moved nearer. "Mayor Langston, are you okay?"

Gregory reluctantly turned around. "I'm fine."

Her brows knitted together in concern. "Are you sure?"

He forced a smile, nodding. "We've had a couple of late nights lately. You deserve the night off."

Mariella grinned and looked relieved. She was a pretty woman and, as far as he knew, unattached. But she wasn't his type, and besides, he valued her too much as an employee—and valued his own reputation too much—to get involved romantically.

"Thanks, Mayor. I'll just leave these phone messages on your desk."

"A parting gift, Mariella? Thanks a lot," he replied in a mock hurt tone, even though he knew it wasn't her fault that all of a sudden he was the most hated man in Bay Point.

She gave him an apologetic smile and cast a worried glance outside. "You'd better leave soon, too. It's clouding up out there."

Gregory glanced over his shoulder and saw fat gray clouds stretching and rolling like rumpled sheets across the late-afternoon sky, just above the horizon.

"You're right," he said, turning back. "A storm is brewing."

"I just hope the rain holds off for practice."

He nodded again. "Have fun, and see you tomorrow."

As soon as Mariella closed the door, Gregory cranked the window shut.

Still, he couldn't take his eyes away from the sky. It could have been his imagination, but it seemed as though the sun gleamed brighter now, ever valiant against the dark clouds. He pressed his palm against the warm glass. The low heat of April was just a kiss of what was to come in a few months, but the light ocean breezes always evened out the hot summer days.

The weather was one of the things he loved most about living in California; the other was being mayor of Bay Point.

He couldn't let anything, or anyone, screw up his plans for the city or for the carousel. People were entitled to their opinions, but the bottom line was that everyone knew things had to change in Bay Point, and he was the only one with the power to do it.

Gregory turned away from the window, slid his trademark black fedora on his head and quickly checked his appearance in the full-length mirror behind his office door.

The entire town was counting on him. He had no choice but to push aside his fears and trust Vanessa… a woman he barely knew.

Chapter 2

The bell on the door tinkled, and Vanessa's head snapped up. No matter how she felt on a particular day, the merry sound always cheered her and made her smile. But when she saw who had entered her shop, her lips drooped into a frown.

In his entire term in office, Mayor Langston had never once set foot in her store. *Why now?* she wondered, her eyes narrowing.

He shut the door, looked about the room and wrinkled his nose.

Didn't the man like flowers? she thought with dismay, watching him walk toward her.

She regarded him coolly while at the same time trying not to gawk. She had to admit that despite what she thought and felt about his politics, Gregory was as breathtaking as a drive down the Pacific coast.

His skin, burnished an even deeper brown from the California sun, held not a bit of shine. He wore a dark gray suit that looked as if it had leaped from the hanger right onto him. It was so clean and perfectly tailored. And though she knew he wasn't much older than she was, he oozed the wisdom and class of powerful men twice her age.

Mrs. Barnell, the widowed owner of Bay Point Bed & Breakfast, was at the counter fussing over her daily floral arrangement. She always had a fresh bouquet in the foyer of her establishment, and even though Vanessa offered to deliver it right to her door, she insisted on picking it up herself. Vanessa suspected the woman was lonely.

"These California poppies are just gorgeous, don't you think?"

Vanessa barely heard Mrs. Barnell's question, so focused was she on Gregory, who was now standing a foot or so behind the elderly woman.

He swept the hat from his head, a careless gesture that also managed to seem purposeful at the same time. It made her knees feel brittle, even though she was standing perfectly straight, and she grasped the edge of the counter to maintain her balance.

"I agree. Utterly gorgeous."

Vanessa parted her lips in shock. Instinctively, she knew that hidden in Gregory's seemingly offhand response was something meant to be discovered by her alone, though she had no way of proving it. In the confines of the small room, his deep bass seemed like a hum, both sustaining and drawing energy, and the vibrations from his tone played low and pleasurably in her belly.

His hazel eyes held hers in a way he had no right to do, and a buzz of heat rose in her cheeks. She discreetly swallowed and her insides lit up, kindled by his intense gaze. It was clear that his comment had nothing to do with California poppies and, strangely, everything to do with her.

Mrs. Barnell turned and her mouth dropped open. "Mayor Langston! I was so busy fooling with these flowers that I didn't hear you come in," she gushed, her smile warm and genuine.

Vanessa's heart beat faster as Gregory approached the counter. He rested one palm on the glass, not too far from her hand, and cleared his throat.

"I'm sorry to interrupt, ladies."

"No need to apologize, Mayor," Mrs. Barnell insisted brightly. She patted her silver-laden black hair. The style, though outdated, was attractive on her and reminded Vanessa of an '80s soap opera where the women were catty and mean.

But Mrs. Barnell wasn't anything like those characters. She was softhearted and kind. Still, her face virtually beamed in the presence of Bay Point's most esteemed political official. It made Vanessa want to gag.

"Right, dear?"

She forced a tight smile. "Absolutely not. What can I do for you, Mayor? As you can see, I'm with a customer."

Vanessa hated to sound so impersonal. Maisie was more than a customer; she was a good friend. But for some reason, she found it exasperating that Maisie was being so nice to the mayor, that she was being the only person she knew how to be. Didn't the woman realize he was trying to destroy Bay Point?

Gregory smiled, his teeth gleaming white and perfect behind lips that held untold secrets.

"I need an arrangement, and I know you're the best florist in town."

Vanessa ignored the flush of heat that spawned in her cheeks and began tying a large purple gingham bow around the vase in front of her. In addition to California poppies, the bouquet held a collection of white roses, baby's breath and leafy sprigs of fresh ferns. She inhaled lightly—the fragrance seemed to infuse her troubled spirit.

So he didn't like flowers, but he wanted a bouquet for someone else. She hoped that Maisie, who was often nosy, would inquire who the lucky woman was. But to her disappointment, she didn't.

"As long as it's not like mine," Mrs. Barnell insisted. "Vanessa makes these special for me, and they're different every day. She is truly a gifted artist."

Vanessa felt Gregory's eyes trace the length of her shoulder-length dark brown hair. Goose pimples broke out on her arms under his careful inspection. She'd recently splurged at the salon and had her stylist add golden-brown highlights. She loved her new look. When he lifted his brow slightly, she knew he did, too. That pleased her, although she didn't know why, and she almost smiled with satisfaction.

He laid his fedora on the counter, stirring the air just enough to softly tickle the fine hairs on her arms.

"I agree, Mrs. Barnell—she's one of Bay Point's greatest treasures."

Vanessa narrowed her eyes again slightly and tightened the bow with a dull snap.

Laying it on a bit thick, aren't we, Mayor?

There was an awkward pause, and it seemed as though Gregory wanted to say more. His towering presence so close to her, with only the counter between them, was distracting in a way she didn't understand.

Vanessa sniffed lightly. Unless her sensitive nose was failing her at the moment, Gregory seemed to be wearing no cologne, and she almost sighed with relief. The musk of male skin was far more pleasing and would require a more careful inspection of him than discreetness would allow. She blushed at the thought, and the glass felt oddly warm against her lower abdomen as she braced herself against it.

Yet Mrs. Barnell didn't seem to notice anything was wrong, and Vanessa was grateful when she slipped her purse over one arm. She turned and regarded Vanessa.

"That's beautiful, dear. I'll be on my way now."

Maisie's toffee-colored skin was a striking contrast to the milky-white vase as she clasped her veined hands around it.

"Need any help with that?" Gregory offered.

Mrs. Barnell shook her head. "These flowers and the walk I take every day to get here are the reasons I'm still active. After my husband, Frank, died…"

Her voice faded away, and she seemed lost in her thoughts. A few seconds later, she straightened her shoulders and looked Gregory up and down.

"It's a shame you're not married."

Vanessa's mouth dropped open slightly at Mrs. Barnell's remark.

Anyone overhearing the conversation and who didn't know her would probably think Maisie was just some old busybody handing out commentary nobody wanted to hear on matters that were none of her business.

But Vanessa knew better. The woman was the unofficial matriarch of Bay Point. Locals deemed anything she said either wacky or wise. Despite her eccentric personality, Mrs. Barnell was well respected in the community.

Gregory dropped his hands and smiled patiently, as if he wasn't at all shocked at her question.

"Right now I think the town needs me more than I need a wife."

Mrs. Barnell nodded. "That we do, Mayor," she agreed, a trace of wistfulness in her voice. She glanced down at the flowers. "But without love, even the most beautiful things can wither away and die."

Vanessa stepped around the counter and said nothing, refusing to let the old woman's words infiltrate her heart. She knew what it was like to live without love, and she was surviving just fine. It was when she was in love that she felt as if she were dying.

As she guided Maisie the short distance to the door, Gregory followed, as though he were afraid neither woman would make it. While she appreciated his consideration, it felt like an imposition, too. She wasn't used to a man like him looking out for her, at least not without wanting something in return.

She kept her eyes focused on the store window, where the name of her beloved shop, Blooms in Paradise, was gracefully scripted in frosted white letters on the glass. She opened the front door and a mildly warm breeze, tinged around the edges with the chill of an impending storm, rushed into the room.

"It looks and feels like it's going to rain any second," said Mrs. Barnell, her teeth chattering slightly. "I'd better hurry."

Vanessa stuck her head outside. "It certainly does. Give me a call when you get home so I know you arrived safely."

When her friend was gone, she swiftly closed the door. The bell was still tinkling as she flipped the small plastic sign over from Open to Closed.

Vanessa took a deep breath before turning and brushing past Gregory, and she could feel his eyes on her back. It warmed and seared her most pleasurably, spine to calves, making her want to run away, a sensory danger sign.

She stopped in front of the two refrigerated cases that protected and displayed her inventory of flowers. Without turning, words tumbled out as if she were in a hurry, even though she had all the time in the world.

"What sort of arrangement do you need, Mayor? If you want something simple, I can put it together for you now. If you want something special, I can have it delivered tomorrow."

She opened the door of one of the cases. The rush of air seemed unusually cold. As she reached in and switched off the fluorescent light for the evening, her nipples hardened.

Vanessa knew she should have worn a padded bra underneath her outfit, but the sheer one was the only one in her collection that was clean. Besides, she'd opened the doors of her flower cases countless times all day, and her breasts had never reacted so obviously before.

Stepping back, Vanessa shut the door and watched his reflection morph in the glass, flattening and changing before her very eyes.

"I don't need flowers, Ms. Hamilton. I need a favor."

Disappointment lodged in her throat. *I knew it.* At the same time, she was oddly euphoric that he wasn't there to buy flowers for another woman.

She quickly turned to face him, her navy maxi skirt swishing around her slim legs and calves.

Gregory's eyes dropped to her cowl-neck blouse. Even with a quick glance down, she could see that the white silky fabric had tented ever so slightly around her nipples.

Her head snapped up and so did his glance, and she blushed.

It's not him. It's the cold air! she told herself.

Though her cheeks burned hot and his lips curved into a playful smile, she brazenly refused to cross her arms and instead placed her hands on her hips. She didn't want him to know she was embarrassed by what he saw, and yet she didn't want to cover up, either.

"What kind of favor? If it's a bodyguard you need, clearly that's not my expertise," she replied, forking a thumb to the case behind her.

"I would imagine that the thorns of a rose would make a pretty good weapon," Gregory replied, and then laughed. "Besides, why would I need a bodyguard?"

She stared at him in disbelief. "I read the *Courier* this morning. The whole town is talking, especially the people who own businesses along Ocean Avenue."

He clasped his hands behind him, turned and walked to the window. "Ah yes, the downtown redevelopment project. And what are the people saying?"

"That you've back-ended them. That you've put

the wheels in motion without any input from the people your plan will be affecting the most."

Gregory heeled around, unclasped his hands and held them palm open against his chest.

"There's been talk about redeveloping downtown for years. I'm only doing what my predecessor always wanted to do but could never seem to get done."

Vanessa shook her head in disgust, opened the second flower case and turned out the lights. Under Gregory's watchful eyes, the refrigerated air in the case seemed even chillier now. Her nipples tightened painfully beneath the silk of her bra, but she no longer cared.

Her spirit drew strength from the colorful blooms, reminding her of what was important.

Protecting her livelihood. That was what mattered.

She closed the door, sealing the air and the flowers for the night. "Passing the buck of blame? Watch it, Mayor Langston," she warned icily, her breath misting against the glass. "You're starting to sound like a politician."

Vanessa saw his reflection move toward her, so she abruptly turned and went behind the counter, grateful for the barrier between them.

Gregory approached and raised an eyebrow. "Mrs. Barnell didn't mention one word about the redevelopment. If anyone would have anything to say, it would be her."

Vanessa stabbed at the buttons on her cash register

until the drawer opened. "Maisie is a kind, decent-hearted woman. Sadly, she has too much respect for you to call you out on what is a sorely misguided plan."

Gregory chuckled, rankling her nerves. "Revitalizing Bay Point's downtown to make it more attractive for everyone is a misguided plan?"

"Don't oversimplify things, Mayor," she snapped, narrowing her eyes. "You're going to tear down some of our beautiful historic downtown buildings and replace them with ugly, tacky condos."

"Lifestyle centers," he corrected.

"Strip malls and overpriced plywood boxes," she shot back. "Both completely devoid of any structural beauty."

"No, Vanessa," Gregory replied in a slow and even tone. "Gorgeous contemporary living spaces where residents have access to everything they need."

Instead of replying, she shook her head and quickly counted the cash and coins in the drawer. Then she grabbed her ledger book from underneath the counter and notated the amount.

Focusing on the task at hand, before too long she'd added up her profit for the day, and she stuffed the cash plus a few checks into a zippered leather envelope. As soon as Gregory left, she was going to walk down to the bank and deposit the meager amount. Then she was going to go home, take a hot bath and try to forget that he was ever here.

"It sounds like a jail to me," she said finally, not looking up at the man.

Gregory cleared his throat. "People want modern amenities and a home with an ocean view," he explained with smooth calmness. "Now they'll get both in Bay Point."

She lifted her eyes and sniffed in annoyance. "Yeah, for a price. You know, most people around here can't afford their own home, let alone buying a new one."

"There will be tax-abatement incentives that will help," he insisted. "And we're partnering with banks that will be willing to lend with little to no down payment."

"It's not enough. And it will never work," she replied with a vehemence that made her proud and sad at the same time. She normally wasn't a negative person. Politicians, even gorgeous ones, seemed to bring out the worst in her.

"It will work," he insisted. "With your help, that is. I want you to be my campaign manager."

She slammed the cash drawer closed, and it felt as if her heart had jumped off a cliff. Although she and Gregory had grown up in the same town, she didn't even know the man, and now he wanted her at his side?

"You must be joking."

Her words came out clipped, but it felt as though they were spoken through mud. Gregory placed both palms on the counter. "I assure you, I'm not."

Vanessa's throat tightened almost painfully, and she could have drowned in the confident intensity of his hazel eyes.

"And I can assure *you* that I'm not interested."

Gregory took a step back. "Really? I'm surprised. Your father told me that flowers are not your only talent. You also have a knack for public relations, and you've been especially successful helping politicians in a crisis, I hear."

Vanessa's stomach burned with resentment. Her father had no business talking to the mayor about her, but she'd deal with him later.

In Gregory's voice, she heard no trace of disdain, and that was good. There were only two people who knew the sordid details of her stint in political public relations, and that was the way it would remain. She was a pro at hiding the secrets of powerful and successful men, and even better at hiding her own.

Vanessa tilted her head. "Oh, so you're admitting your reelection campaign is in trouble?"

"Not trouble," he insisted, lifting one finger. "Just a bit of a rough spot."

She broached a wry smile. "I'd say you're at the top of a raging waterfall about to crash to the rocks below."

Gregory leaned in closer. "I like to live dangerously," he murmured in a low voice.

At his words, her pulse raced anew, chasing something elusive and sensual.

She was relieved when he stepped away from the counter and peered into one of the refrigerated cases.

"How's business been lately?"

It sucks, she thought as she took a sip from her water bottle. But she wasn't going to tell him that. Had he seen the ledger? She wished she'd waited until he was gone to count the cash drawer.

"Steady. I can't complain."

That much was true. Between her walk-in customers, internet orders and those from the hospital, Blooms in Paradise was just breaking even. She hadn't had a paycheck in months, though, so she was teaching a floral design class at a community college the next town over just to make ends meet. Still, the bills were piling up with no end in sight, and her emergency savings account was almost tapped out.

"Steady," he repeated to the glass. "That's good, but growth is even better."

"At least it's reliable," she retorted, and thought she saw his shoulders twitch back.

She hadn't meant her words to be a slam against him, but when she quickly thought about it, maybe she did. Why couldn't he just let things in Bay Point stay the same? Sure, things were rough now, but the economy was on the upswing. People would start shopping and eating downtown again. Tourists would rediscover Bay Point's charm.

Wouldn't they?

Vanessa squeezed her bottle of water until the

plastic crunched loudly. Gregory faced her and opened his mouth, but no words came out.

She felt her blood pressure rise and readied herself for an argument, but he simply turned and walked over to the window.

From where she stood, she knew he was looking at Lucy's Bar and Grille. Located directly across the street from her shop, it was the only remaining restaurant on downtown Ocean Avenue. All the others had either closed or moved somewhere else.

Gregory chuckled, the sound strangely poignant. "When I was little, my father and I had dinner at Lucy's often, especially when my mom was in Washington trying to drum up support for her latest cause."

"She was a lobbyist, correct?"

"She still is." He nodded, his back ramrod straight. "Anyway, most nights it was so crowded the only reason we got a seat was because we always had a reserved table."

He turned to Vanessa, and his expression was difficult for her to read.

"I guess it pays to be one of the richest families in town," she mused.

His eyes found hers, and she was surprised at the whisper of guilt that crossed his face.

"Those were the good old days," he said, as if he didn't hear her.

Vanessa skirted around the counter, hoping to put an end to his walk down memory lane. Sometimes the past wasn't meant to be revisited—it was meant to be forgotten.

"What are you talking about? The Langstons are still one of the wealthiest families in Bay Point. Nothing has changed for you."

She faced him, folding her arms across her chest. Her body was still heated, but not from desire, from anger.

"If you're so concerned with memories, what about the Bay Point Carousel?" she accused. "Don't you know what it means to the community?"

He didn't answer, but a scowl crossed his face, and she wondered why.

"The carousel is part of our town's history," she continued. "You can't tear it down!"

He turned and leaned against the counter. "I have to do what I think is best for Bay Point."

Her heart sank, but she remained undeterred. "Are you looking for a vote of approval for your plan? Because you don't have mine, and you never will."

He stared at her a moment, and she thought she saw a flash of hurt in his eyes.

"You don't have to agree with the redevelopment. I just need you to help me convince everyone else in Bay Point. Despite what you think, I am trying to make things better."

His earnestness almost made Vanessa believe him. But she knew from past experience that guys like him, with their good looks and charm, could suck the heart and independence from a woman. He'd do the very same thing to Bay Point.

"By destroying the legacy of the place you and I grew up in?" she railed. "Somehow I missed that part of your campaign speech, and so did the rest of the town."

His eyes widened slightly, and he picked up his hat from the counter. She thought he was going to put it on and leave, but then he put it down again.

"Like the carousel, many of the homes are dilapidated and in need of repair. They're an eyesore on the community."

The determination in his voice, measured and even, tried to convince her of the practicality of his statement. It also appeared to be a veiled warning that there was no way she could change his mind.

"Those 'eyesores' have been in the respective owners' families and in this community for generations," Vanessa countered.

She crossed her arms, determined to be just as practical and just as stubborn. "Now you're going to raze them, and you expect me to help you? Get real, Mayor."

Gregory moved toward her. "You've got it all wrong."

He touched her shoulder with one fingertip. She jumped back in surprise, but it was too late. The brief contact had already leached a single pulse of fire into her bare skin.

"Whatever you have to say, I don't want to hear it."

"You'll want to hear this."

She found it hard to avoid his eyes, so gentle yet commanding attention.

"You remember when we used to play together, right? When we were kids?"

"It was one time, Mayor. Just once."

"Right. Anyway, remember how we were making mud patties in the back of your grandma's yard?" he continued, a grin on his face. "I'd water the dirt, and you'd stir it all together with a stick until the ground turned all wet and gooey. Then we'd take our shoes off, step in and squish the mud between our toes. And you'd laugh and laugh."

"Yeah, so?" she replied, keeping her expression and her tone light.

His lips curved up. "Whether or not you decide to manage my campaign, I'd pay any price to see you smile like that again."

Her stomach dropped as if she'd just plummeted over a steep hill, yet she managed to ignore the feeling. She brushed past him and opened the door of her shop.

"Leave and I'll smile for free."

Gregory turned back to the counter and grabbed his hat. Her eyes settled on the collar of his crisp white shirt, his trim waist and then his pants, which fit nicely over his backside.

He stopped in front of her. When he slid his hat onto his head, it took everything in her power not to take a step back. Though her feet remained rooted to the floor, she felt drawn to him, like a young seedling yearning toward the sky. She could wilt like a flower against him—probably lots of women could and did, but not her.

"Too bad I won't be around to see it," he said softly.

Gregory looked into her eyes, and once again she found it difficult to look away.

"Come on, Vanessa. You remember what Bay Point used to be like when we were in school."

She sniffed. "I barely knew you then, and I don't know you now. So don't even act like we were friends, Mayor."

Gregory laughed. "You act as though we Langstons were kings and everyone else in Bay Point were our serfs. You know that's not true. Your father was, and still is, a well-respected physician. You certainly weren't poor," he pointed out.

"Leave my father—and my family—out of this."

The frostiness in her tone was unwarranted, and she knew Gregory wasn't accusing her. Still, his statement galled her. Her family might not have been poor, but they also never had the air of entitlement cloaked around them that the Langston family always had. Or at least, Gregory's mother and father.

Gregory's expression sobered again as he plucked one of the red roses from the fresh bouquet she always kept by the door.

"Look, neither of us have any control over our

backgrounds, but together you and I could bring back the magic of Bay Point."

He ran the barely open bud along her jawline, arousing her tender skin until it felt as if it were on fire. She bit the inside of her lip as the heady scent wafted toward her nose, seeming to swirl like a dervish around her head.

"Think about my offer, Vanessa. You won't regret it."

Gregory gently tapped the bud on her chin, just once. It was enough to make her throat go dry and wish it were his lips.

He bowed slightly and left, taking the rose with him.

She locked the door, then carefully gathered up the remaining roses and walked over to the refrigerated case. One by one, she placed the stems inside an empty vase. When she was finished, she closed the door and placed her palm against the glass.

She stared at the bouquet of roses. Twelve had become eleven, and she felt as though she'd lost some kind of intimate battle. A war within herself—a war she was tired of fighting.

"We can't live in the past, Gregory," she said softly, her warm breath misting against the glass. "But we can't completely erase it, either."

Ever since she was a child, she'd always felt safe in the garden. Or now as an adult in her shop. Tending to her flowers. As if they could hide her from anyone, protect her from anything. Help her to re-member. Make her forget.

That time was gone. So was her sense of security.

When, Vanessa wondered sadly, had everything changed?

Chapter 3

At 8:00 a.m. the next morning, Gregory angled his car into an empty parking spot on Ocean Avenue in front of city hall and slowly got out. He half expected an angry mob to be waiting there to carry him off to the gallows. But except for a few seagulls strutting about as if the world owed them a meal, the wide stone steps were empty.

He slammed the door, exhaling a breath he wasn't even aware he was holding. Clutching his briefcase, he quickly jogged up the stairs, sending the birds squawking and scattering into the cool salty air.

His eyes crinkled behind his sunglasses. How could Vanessa have turned down his offer to be his campaign manager? He still couldn't believe it, nor could he believe how much she'd changed physically.

Back when he was a prepubescent nine-year-old, somewhere in his psyche, where he involuntarily noticed these things because he was a boy and she was a girl, Gregory had thought she was cute. Yucky, but cute. She liked making mud pies, and that was beyond cool.

But somewhere along the way, when he was off at college and then working at his father's law firm, she'd grown up to be beautiful. A fact that he'd always known, since he saw her from a distance around Bay Point quite often. Her flower shop was only a few minutes on foot from city hall. However, he'd never truly realized how absolutely stunning she was until yesterday, when he was in the same room with her.

It was everything—her lustrous brown hair, streaked in gold, the hint of the curve of her breasts, the innocent pucker of her nipples covered by the silky fabric of her blouse and the long legs well hidden beneath her skirt, which might as well have been a nun's habit.

His groin tightened painfully again, as it had been doing ever since last night each time he thought about her.

Vanessa Hamilton was as dangerous to his career as raising property taxes, but she was also necessary to it. He'd spent a long, restless night attempting to figure out a way to change her mind. Instead he'd awoken with a massive hard-on and no solid ideas.

The shouts and screams of toddlers broke through

his yawn-sodden thoughts. He turned around and frowned.

Directly across from city hall, the Bay Point Carousel beckoned him like an aging beauty. "Ride me! Ride me!" it seemed to urge. Although the paint on the horses was dull and chipped, the mirrors cracked and the jewels dusty and worn, the carousel held an undeniable fire of mystery. One that he was happy to extinguish. So much so that razing the carousel was in phase one of his downtown redevelopment plan.

He shook his head, recalling how Vanessa had gotten all bent out of shape that he was going to tear the ancient structure down. Although he didn't know for sure, the carousel seemed to be more to her than just a relic of Bay Point's history. A small part of him wanted to know why, but the other part of him couldn't wait to get rid of the town's "legacy," which held nothing but bad memories for him.

Besides, politics always trumped preservation. Everybody knew that, he told himself, and promptly dismissed the guilt that suddenly bubbled within him from out of nowhere. The carousel would be replaced with a beautiful garden, a contemporary fountain and green spaces that would be free of insurance liability issues and high maintenance costs.

"Everyone's going to love it, including Vanessa!" he muttered to himself. With or without her, somehow he'd have to convince the citizens of Bay Point that his plan was the right thing to do.

He turned away and entered the building through

the revolving doors. The cool air engulfed him, and he shivered a little as he nodded at the security guard. Then he took the elevator to the fourth floor, where his office was located.

"Good morning, Mariella."

"Morning, Mayor." She jerked a thumb toward his open door. "Mr. Stodwell is here to see you, and he's in your office." She dropped her voice low. "I'm sorry. I told him that you prefer visitors to wait out here, but he ignored me and barged right in."

"It's okay," he assured her. "How was soccer practice?"

Mariella's face beamed with surprise. "Great. It was only a scrimmage match, but Josh scored his first goal of the season!"

"That's great. Maybe he's another Beckham in the works, and we'll finally have a winning team in Bay Point." He put his fingers to his lips. "But don't tell Coach Perkins I said so, because he thinks the only ball that should be in play in this town is a football."

Mariella giggled. "Your secret is safe with me. There's fresh coffee. Want some?"

"How many cups has Mr. Stodwell had?"

Mariella held up two fingers, and he shook his head. "Then I'd better ace this one alone—without the help of caffeine."

Gregory opened his office door. Mr. Stodwell gestured toward the window with his coffee cup. "Those kids out there. Where do they get their energy?"

Gregory laid his briefcase on his desk and snapped

it open, revealing the rose from Vanessa's shop. He'd forgotten he'd put it there, and he quickly closed the briefcase before Stodwell spotted it. He still didn't know why he'd kept the now-wilted bud, other than the fact that the petals had once touched her skin. He wished it had been his fingers instead.

"I'm sure the sugar fixes don't help," Gregory offered.

Ruby's Tasty Pastries, located on the other side of Ocean Avenue and across from the carousel, was known for its doughnuts that were shaped like lions, tigers and bears for kids, and other rich, butter-laden delights for adults. The organic coffee and beverages were also quite popular among the townspeople.

Mr. Stodwell grunted and patted his belly. "Ruby's doughnuts just make me even fatter. But I love them and eat them anyway."

He took a handkerchief out of his front pocket. Like a cold glass of water in the hot sun, the man always seemed to be perspiring. He wiped his brow before plopping his large frame down on the wooden chair in front of Gregory's desk.

Gregory sat down, and as usual, his chair squeaked noisily. He couldn't wait until the new city hall was built. The first thing he was going to do was buy a new chair. Until then, to save costs, he put up with the old one.

"I don't think we had a meeting scheduled, but now that you're here, I have to tell you how disappointed I and the rest of the planning commission

were to see the news about the redevelopment project in the *Bay Point Courier* yesterday."

Mr. Stodwell shrugged. "I called in a few favors—
so what?" he replied, sounding quite pleased with
himself. "Besides, it's not like folks didn't know that
this was coming. Small towns run on rumors like
these."

Gregory wrinkled his brow in annoyance. "I
thought we'd talked about waiting to announce the
redevelopment plan until I'd had a chance to discuss
the proposal with the stakeholders."

Stodwell coughed, and a bit of coffee sloshed on
his shirt, but he didn't seem to notice.

"What's the big deal? Now the news is out and
in the open. Folks that have businesses downtown
know that their time is almost up. Bay Point, as we
know it now, will be forever changed."

Gregory abruptly stood and leaned over his desk.
"The big deal," he replied curtly, "is that you blindsided me. And now the town thinks I blindsided
them."

Including Vanessa.

"I grew up with some of the people affected. Need
I remind you that I am up for reelection in a few
months?"

Stodwell shrugged. "I don't see the problem. You
own the land. You have all the cards here."

"The city owns the land," Gregory corrected.
"Not me."

"Minor detail," Stodwell said, waving two fingers. "Anyway, I've got some good news."

He paused and swabbed his handkerchief over his cheeks. "I'm ready to sell the buildings I own downtown to you—I mean the city of Bay Point."

Gregory raised his eyebrows in surprise. Stodwell had been on the fence for months about releasing his properties, even though Gregory had hinted that the city might be interested in purchasing them. Now it looked as though they would get the chance.

"That's good to hear. You own most of the buildings alongside Ocean Avenue, except for a few owned by Mrs. Barnell. Why did you decide to sell now?"

Although his buildings were old, they were still valuable. If the downtown redevelopment plan was as successful as Gregory hoped it would be, the buildings and the land they sat on would eventually be worth tens of millions of dollars.

Stodwell edged his body forward. "It's the right time for me, and for the city."

Gregory nodded. The man was right. If the city owned the buildings outright, it would make the redevelopment process a whole lot easier.

Stodwell leaned back in his chair. "Besides, some of my tenants haven't paid rent on time, or at all, in months. Because of that, I can't make repairs or upgrade the buildings or the apartments upstairs."

"Why didn't you ever sue the tenants for the money?"

"Are you kidding?" Stodwell widened his eyes in mock horror. "I gotta live here, too, Mayor. I could have shook 'em down for the money, but that's not my style."

Gregory barely held back a smirk. "So now you want us to do it, is that right?"

Stodwell opened both palms, his grin like a swath of grease on his tanned face. "I have to assume if they're not paying me, they're not paying the city, either. Am I right?"

Gregory frowned and didn't respond. As in most cities, businesses had to pay a yearly tax to operate in Bay Point, although some exemptions did apply.

Six months ago, he'd had an independent audit conducted of Bay Point's finances. The third-party firm had discovered that there was nearly a quarter of a million dollars in unpaid business taxes that were not in the city's coffers, which was one reason why the city was in a financial mess.

"Once the city owns all the properties, you can call a lien on each one of them." Stodwell clapped his hands. "Problem solved."

Gregory immediately thought of Vanessa. "I can't do that. There has to be a better solution."

Stodwell shrugged. "Threaten eviction, and people suddenly get very creative about paying up."

Gregory held back a gasp. Throw his fellow residents out on the streets? He could never live with himself. He'd grown up with most of the store owners.

It would be difficult enough collecting back taxes

from them. In light of the economy and the lack of
tourists, Stodwell's business tenants were having a
hard time staying profitable. How would they come
up with the extra money for back taxes and rent in-
creases? He could never evict them.

"Neither I nor the city is willing to go that far,"
he said firmly. "Besides, it's—"

"Election time. I know."

Stodwell slurped down the rest of his coffee and
set it on the desk.

"You need me, Gregory. And I need…a very nice
retirement. I am willing to sell the properties to the
city. If you don't want to deal with them, sell them
to the developer."

"I'm not even sure if he'd be willing to buy them,"
Gregory said.

"That'll be your problem, not mine." Stodwell
twisted a wide gold ring on his finger. "I left a re-
port with your assistant of how much is owed to me
by various tenants. Obviously, those monies will be
included in the selling price, which the city can re-
coup however, and whenever, it wishes."

Gregory thought for a moment. "I need time to
review everything and discuss it with city council."

"You have sixty days."

Gregory quickly glanced down at his desk cal-
endar.

Stodwell grinned. "Don't worry. The deadline
falls after the election. I'm doing you a favor, Mayor.
I could sell outright to the developer." He lifted his

hands and shrugged. "Though I'd make far less money on the deal because—"

"They would be less likely to buy at your asking price because of all the repairs that need to be done," Gregory concluded.

"Exactly. When I realized that you intended to keep most of the downtown buildings intact, that's when I made the decision to sell and get out now, while I could still make a little bit of profit, and the city can still make good use of them."

Gregory nodded, even though Stodwell's comment irked him. He knew the man didn't care a bit about Bay Point. He was just out to make a fast buck, and it was up to Gregory to make sure that he wasn't going to do it at Bay Point's expense.

"We'll have to see if we can work your buildings into the development and construction schedule," Gregory reasoned.

"Are you still going to tear the carousel down first?"

"Yes, plus, a few other buildings will be razed to make way for new condos and town houses, as part of the multiuse lifestyle center that will be built. The rest will remain, and the exteriors will be renovated. If the city buys your properties, we can perhaps schedule the renovations in phase two."

Stodwell nodded. "This redevelopment idea of yours. It's a good plan, Mayor. One that will far outlive you and me combined. I urge you and city council to consider my offer."

Gregory leaned his hip against his desk. "I can't guarantee that we will be able to purchase the properties at the price you want. I have to be mindful of the budget."

"All I can do is ask, Mayor. If we can't do a deal, I'm sure the developer will be interested in this opportunity. But if he buys it, you'd lose some measure of control over what happens with the buildings, other than what's covered under existing commercial zoning regulations, of course."

Gregory's heart suddenly constricted in his chest. Stodwell owned the building that Vanessa's flower shop was in, as well as Lucy's Bar and Grille and some others in the same block. He knew the day was coming when he'd have to oversee the collection process of all the past-due business taxes, and he was dreading it. Plus, he knew that city council would likely want to raise rents to help cover the costs of purchasing Stodwell's commercial properties.

Both would drastically affect his popularity with Bay Point voters.

"I just want to be sure that the residents and store owners will not suffer undue harm. I wanted to gain their trust before—"

Stodwell held up a pudgy hand. "Wait a minute. They elected you the mayor of Bay Point. You already earned their trust four years ago."

"And I don't want to lose it, either."

The man laughed. "You've got a lot of things to learn about politics, son."

"That may be so, but how to piss off my constituency is not one of them."

"When they see the end result, they won't be mad. In fact, I'm willing to bet that they'll thank you." Stodwell paused a moment. "Need I remind you of the donation made to your campaign by my company?"

Gregory clenched his stomach muscles in disgust. He hated being made to feel as if he could be bought. It was the one thing he despised about politics.

"Your support is graciously appreciated."

Stodwell stood. "You know, Gregory, your father and I go back a long ways. It would be a shame if you lost this election."

"I don't plan on losing," he said, forcing his tone to be relaxed.

He watched Stodwell wrest his chubby arms into his too-small suit jacket, a visual reminder of the dangers of eating too many doughnuts.

"Well, Mayor. I'm glad to hear you're so confident. But sometimes the best-laid plans have a quirky way of going awry."

The two men shook hands.

"I'll be in touch," Gregory said, and closed the door behind him.

He walked over to the window, pressed his forehead against the glass and stared down at the carousel. The damn thing never worked now, but it ran fine when he was a kid.

Back when he dreamed about riding it. When he

thought just one ride would make his well-to-do family normal, not a constant source of envy or gossip.

He turned away from the window and punched the intercom button. "Mariella, please bring me the list of people who owe commercial-business-related taxes."

When he'd originally received the list several weeks ago, he hadn't paid very close attention to the names on it.

Now there was one name he hoped he wouldn't see: Vanessa's.

Chapter 4

That same day, Vanessa ducked into Lucy's and slid into one of the empty bright blue booths facing the window. She looked around and nodded to a few folks who were already seated for lunch. Thankfully, the mayor wasn't one of them.

She put her cell phone on vibrate before stowing it away in her purse. Although she couldn't run from Gregory forever, at least she could avoid his calls. If she picked up, no doubt he would try to persuade her to change her mind about managing his election campaign. It would be easy to tell him no on the phone. But in person? Vanessa wasn't sure she could do that again.

She'd always been attracted to powerful men. But it wasn't long before she discovered, often painfully, that under their shiny veneer of success, most of them weren't very nice people to be around.

Vanessa had a feeling that Gregory was different. He didn't look at her as if she were someone to be conquered. He didn't try to impress her with his credentials or his bank account. Although maybe that didn't count, because the whole town knew that he'd graduated with honors from Stanford and that his family was one of the wealthiest in Bay Point.

Instead he had reminded her of a childhood memory, one she'd long forgotten. The two of them playing together, making mud pies. And for a moment, she'd remembered what it was like to be free, unencumbered by daily responsibilities, an ever-growing mound of bills and tough choices.

He remembered my smile.

Her heart skipped a beat—

And yet he wants to destroy the carousel.

—then sank in her chest like a rock.

The Bay Point Carousel was the hub of downtown. Vehicles had to navigate around it to get to Magnolia Avenue north- or southbound or to continue west on Ocean Avenue. Parking spots jutted out on all sides like the spokes of a bicycle wheel. Right now there were only a few minivans in front, likely parents bringing their children to play, even though it currently wasn't operational.

Vanessa peered out the window. The structure was about a block away, and though she could see only a horse or two, it was enough to stir a flood of memories, most of them happy.

She planted her elbows on the mint-green laminate table. The carousel meant so much to her and the people of Bay Point. Why didn't it mean anything to the mayor?

And why do I care? She nearly said that thought aloud, but instead she pursed her lips and let out a slow breath.

The aromatic scent of incense and coffee beans wafted over her. She lifted her head just as Lucy Dee Diller, owner of the diner, set down a shiny aluminum carafe.

"What's wrong, child? Rough morning?"

Vanessa nodded but chose not to mention the tall, dark and handsome half of her troubles.

"I had a bunch of deliveries to Bay Point Hospital and a few nursing homes in the area. It's hard to see so many sick and elderly people."

Lucy turned over a white porcelain cup and nestled it into its accompanying saucer. "Your flowers will make them feel better, no?"

Vanessa bit her lip and rubbed her palms on her khaki pants. She felt a trail of sweat bead at the base of her spine beneath her white polo, emblazoned just above her left breast with the shop's logo.

"I guess..." She trailed off.

Although there were many patients who were on the road back to recovery, her mind always seemed to return to the ones who weren't so lucky. She didn't want to tell Lucy how many times she'd delivered a cheery get-well floral arrangement to an individual at the hospital and a few days later delivered a more somber arrangement to the patient's family at a funeral home.

In her darkest moods, she sometimes wondered how flowers could make a difference. But deep down, she knew that they did because of the life-changing effect they'd had on her own life.

"I just wish I could do more. Sometimes I feel so powerless."

"Ah...perhaps you need to rub the crystal ball more often?"

Vanessa skirted her eyes over to the large glass orb nestled on a gold-columned pedestal near the front of the store. People routinely touched or patted it on their way out of the restaurant for good luck. Being a tad germophobic and a nonbeliever in Lucy's magic mumbo jumbo, she never indulged.

But maybe, she thought, *I should start.*

She grinned. "Couldn't hurt." Then her smile faltered. "What does your crystal ball say about the future of Bay Point?"

Lucy sighed heavily. "Change is never easy."

She poured Vanessa some coffee, then slid into the opposite side of the booth.

"When I came to Bay Point from New Orleans to open my diner, I was twenty-two and full of California dreams. The sun...the surf...the men." She giggled. "It was a different era."

Vanessa's eyes widened. "What was the town like back then?"

Lucy folded her hands like a prim schoolgirl, but her eyes held a devilish gleam. "On weekends it was like a mini Hollywood. Lots of stars would drive up the coast from Los Angeles or Beverly Hills. Beautiful women. Gorgeous men. Actors, actresses and directors seeking their escape from the production lot and the photographers."

"Didn't the paparazzi follow them?"

"No. They weren't as aggressive back then as they are now. Besides, the stars were always in disguise, which they promptly took off once they arrived here safely."

Vanessa mused. "Disguises?"

Lucy chuckled at the memory. "A man might dress as a rabbi, a woman as a nun. Nothing too complicated, but they were actors. They could pull anything off."

Vanessa glanced around at the walls, where some autographed photos hung alongside porcelain signs, Cajun art and other antique treasures Lucy had brought from her native Louisiana. The entire place had an irresistible charm.

"I'm amazed no one ratted them out to the highest bidder."

"The tabloids—we used to call them *the rags*," Lucy confided, "would call some of the store owners, including me, but to my knowledge, no one ever bit."

"People were respectful of their privacy," Vanessa concluded.

Lucy nodded. "We all knew that they'd come here for rest and relaxation. There's no crime in that, and no need to bring it to anyone's attention."

She laughed heartily and leaned closer. "Lord, they used to love my jerk chicken."

"We all still do!" Vanessa affirmed. "Mayor Langston claims the redevelopment project will bring more tourist dollars into Bay Point. How do you feel about that?"

Lucy shrugged. "Their money is just as green as ours and—"

"But at the expense of our historic buildings? Although I haven't seen the drawings, I'm betting that his so-called contemporary lifestyle center is butt ugly."

Lucy leaned back against the booth. "Ah…if that is true, our mayor has the looks of a movie star, but his brains must be temporarily lost at sea." She patted Vanessa's hand. "At any rate, I think our stores are safe. The mayor can't do anything unless George Stodwell sells his properties to the city. And you know how stubborn he is."

Vanessa made a face. "Yeah, I have to twist his arm to make any repairs. I've had a leak in my bathroom ceiling for two months! Do you think he ever sent anyone out to fix it?"

Lucy smirked. "I know why he hasn't been over

here to do anything, except to gobble up my food for free."

"Why free? He has more than enough money to pay!"

"It's the least I can do. I'm behind on my rent. I've told him I'm working on getting the money, but business hasn't been so good lately."

She folded her hands on the table, and Vanessa could see them trembling. "And I don't need my crystal ball to tell me what's coming."

At Lucy's words, a sliver of fear coursed through Vanessa. She could still pay the rent…barely. But if things didn't turn around soon, she could lose her apartment and the store. Mr. Stodwell didn't seem the type who could be appeased with a dozen roses.

"Don't give up yet," she begged, trying to convince herself as much as her friend.

Lucy gave her a reassuring smile. "I'm not. That's why I'm not too upset about this redevelopment plan. If it can help me save my restaurant, then why shouldn't I be all for it?"

Deep down, Vanessa knew she had a point, but she didn't like the way the mayor was going about it.

"Even so, he should have involved us from the very beginning. I know other business owners feel the same way," Lucy commented.

Vanessa sipped her coffee. Hadn't she told Gregory the very same thing? "I know. I think this is really going to affect his reelection campaign."

Lucy nodded. "Mayor Langston is a fine man and

I'd hate to see him lose, but I think Jacob Billingsly has a real chance right now."

"What are you hearing?"

"Billingsly is going around telling everyone that if he's elected, he'll stop the redevelopment plan."

"Vote Billingsly for mayor," Vanessa mocked, waving her hands. "Because I'm the best and you're not!"

Lucy laughed. "That's not his slogan, and you know it."

Vanessa wrinkled her nose. "It might as well be. The man is a complete tool. Did you read the *Courier* this morning? He's saying it's a huge mistake and that the mayor will ruin the city, blah, blah, blah."

"Don't you feel the same way, Vanessa?"

"Yes… No," she waffled. "I mean, I don't know."

"I'm sure at least some folks will jump on the Billingsly bandwagon, in spite of their loyalty to Mayor Langston and the Langston family overall."

Vanessa tensed at Lucy's words as the sense that she needed to do something to protect Gregory came out of nowhere.

The man can take care of himself.

But even though she instinctively knew that was true, for some reason she had a strong desire to be beside him, to be there if he did fall. It didn't make any sense to her, but the feeling was there, needling at her insides.

If Billingsly became mayor, he could turn around and change things, too. Why would he care about

Bay Point? He didn't even have a history with the town. She wasn't quite sure why he was running for mayor.

"Mayor Langston asked me to be his campaign manager," Vanessa blurted.

Lucy raised an eyebrow. "And?"

"I refused, of course. I'm not going to be party to him destroying downtown Bay Point."

Lucy poured herself a cup of coffee and thought a moment. "But perhaps you could be the one to save it."

"What do you mean?"

"If you were the mayor's campaign manager, you would have the inside scoop at all times with the re-development project."

"So? That doesn't mean I would have any way of changing things."

"Maybe not, but we'd have more of a chance to fight this with someone on the inside."

"I thought you didn't care one way or the other."

"Oh, I care," Lucy reassured her. "I'm just being realistic. You could be a very positive influence on the mayor."

"But isn't it a little dishonest? It's almost like you're suggesting I be an inside informant."

"No. Not at all. Here's what you do," Lucy instructed. "You go to the mayor. You tell him you will be his campaign manager on one condition. That you will be able to act as an advocate for him and for small-business owners at the same time."

Vanessa fiddled with one of the gold hoops that hung from her ears.

"I don't know, Lucy."

"What are you afraid of? I know you managed some kinds of campaigns in Los Angeles before you came back home."

Vanessa cringed inwardly. She had managed campaigns for political officials, but they were more reputation-based crisis communications rather than help in getting someone elected. Plus, she normally worked behind the scenes, and while she was successful, the long hours and the stress of the campaign often turned her clients into lovers. The last one had nearly broken her heart, but not her spirit.

That was why she'd escaped from that world of sex and money and power and returned to the peace of Bay Point. She wasn't about to get involved with another gorgeous man in trouble.

"Let me tell you a little story." Lucy leaned against the table. "When I was a child in New Orleans, my mother had a garden that attracted a lot of butterflies, but I was afraid of them. So I'd press my nose against the window and watch them and wish that I had the courage to go outside. She always told me that little wings can make big waves."

"What did she mean?" Vanessa asked.

"Take a chance, because if you don't, you might miss something beautiful."

Though there was something about Lucy's story that made her want to cry, Vanessa managed a smile.

"If you don't know what to do about the mayor, at least you know how to eat. I'll get you one of my jerk chicken sandwiches, and you can take it with you."

"Thanks, Lucy!" she replied, her stomach rumbling, just about on cue.

She checked her watch. It was almost time to open up the shop. On Fridays, she made her deliveries in the morning and didn't open up Blooms in Paradise until noon.

Lucy came back a few minutes later. The spicy scent of her sandwich leaked through the white paper bag, and Vanessa couldn't wait to dig in. She shouldered her purse, slid out of the booth and hugged her friend. On her way out, and after making sure that no one was looking, she quickly rubbed her hand over the restaurant's famous crystal ball.

Out on the sidewalk, Vanessa glanced down the street at the carousel. It was completely obscured by a delivery truck that was rudely parked across five parking spaces.

But she didn't need a clear view. She had her memories.

Good, happy memories. The type that burbled to the top when things were tough. Memories worth remembering, and definitely worth fighting for.

Chapter 5

By the time Vanessa closed down the shop, it was nearly six o'clock. She didn't know what the mayor's official working hours were, but hopefully, he hadn't gone home yet.

She hurried down Ocean Avenue toward city hall, admiring the structure's neoclassic architecture. The huge columns had never seemed foreboding to her before, but today was different.

She started to perspire a little as she trotted up the stone steps, telling herself that there was no reason to be nervous. Going head-to-head with Gregory Langston was not going to be easy, but she hoped he would at least listen to what she had to say.

Pushing her way through the old revolving door, she still could not believe how easy it was to access

Bay Point's main governmental building. No iden-
tification was required, and there were no weapons
checks, as there were at Los Angeles City Hall. In
Bay Point everyone already knew your name, your
face and most of your business, so there was no need
for the extra intrusion.

It wasn't easy to hide much of anything. A fact
that she loved and hated at the same time.

Vanessa cleared her throat. "Hey, Prentice? How
goes it?"

The elderly security guard and former deacon
of Bay Point Baptist Church was legendary for his
slightly off-color and mostly harmless outlook on
life. A few years ago, he'd told a dirty joke in the
middle of a church service and had been promptly
relieved of his religious duties. Now his time was
spent doing crosswords, directing residents to various departments within the building and jawing with
members of the Bay Point Police and Fire Department, many of whom told dirtier jokes than he could
ever dream up.

Prentice barely raised his eyes, and Vanessa suspected he'd been napping.

"I can still make water standing up without
holding on to a railing, so I guess everything's just
dandy."

"Uh…good to know. I guess," she stammered
awkwardly. "Is the mayor in?"

"I haven't seen him go out." Prentice looked up,

his voice gruff. "And I've kept my eyes peeled on those elevator doors all day."

Vanessa held back a giggle. "Wow. You can see through closed eyelids. That's quite a talent."

"Watch your tongue, missy," Prentice warned with a stern waggle of his bushy eyebrows. "I may not be a churchgoing man anymore, but I do know that 'respect your elders' is still in the Bible."

"I'm sorry, Prentice. I didn't mean any harm. Why don't you come down to my shop tomorrow, and I'll make you up a nice boutonniere. It would look real sharp on your uniform."

"Booty-what?" he joked, and picked up the phone. "You want me to tell him you're here?"

She took a few steps to the elevator and jabbed at the up button. The doors opened immediately. "No. He's expecting me," she lied, stepping in.

Prentice grunted and put the phone back on the receiver, then immediately leaned back and closed his eyes.

Vanessa smiled as she pushed the button for the fourth floor.

"Thanks anyway!" she called out as the elevator doors creaked closed, but Prentice didn't move a muscle.

On the way up, she smoothed her hands down her body, trying to erase the wrinkles from her tan khakis. At least there were no dirt or water spots today. She wished she had changed into something else before meeting with the mayor, but there was no time.

Why should you care what he thinks about you? she chided herself as she stepped out of the elevator and entered a hallway lined with photographs of prior mayors.

As she made her way down the hall, the floor groaned and creaked, even though she was walking lightly. In some places, the walls were cracked with mini fissures. Glancing up, her eyes widened at the water stains on the ceiling. It appeared that the mayor's claim that a new city hall was drastically needed was true. This particular floor seemed in dire need of repair.

The last time she was in city hall was when she moved back to Bay Point. Like many of the stores still in business in Bay Point, Blooms in Paradise had a long history in the town. It was previously owned by her mother and, prior to that, her grandmother. So even though the shop had had a business license, she'd had to get it transferred to her name when she took it over.

The licensing office was on the first floor of the building. It wasn't fancy, but at least it wasn't falling apart. She'd never been up on the fourth floor, and she was surprised at the decay.

Outside his office there was a small desk. It was neat, tidy and devoid of papers. There was a framed photograph of a woman with her arm clasped around a small boy in a soccer uniform holding a little trophy. Both were smiling. A mother's pride. A son's win.

Vanessa took a deep breath and knocked on the door.

"Mariella, I thought I told you that you could go home."

The heavy wooden door may have muffled the mayor's voice, but not the brute sexiness of it. Warm and dark, it was like a sudden kiss or a whiff of spicy cologne. Her heart pounded in her chest. What would it sound like close to her ear or against the inside of her thighs?

"It's not Mariella, Mayor. It's Vanessa Hamilton."

She bent her ear to the door and stepped a bit closer. A chair scraped against the floor. The quick shuffling of papers. And heavy, determined footsteps, which made her wonder idly about his shoe size. She almost started to giggle when the door suddenly opened. The force of the air whooshed back the tendrils of hair framing her face.

Gregory crossed his arms, and Vanessa nearly gulped. His biceps were not popping out of his dress shirt, but she could sense their powerful strength nonetheless.

His sleeves were rolled up, just below his elbow. A gold watch on his right wrist was a stark contrast to his dark skin.

"Ms. Hamilton. This is a pleasant surprise."

His voice waved over her, brisk and smooth, then lowered and turned into something else.

Something meant just for her.

"Have you come to grant me the smile I wished for all last night?"

He thought about me?

Her stomach took a surprise dive at his teasing words, but she had no trouble meeting his eyes.

She forced her lips into a firm line. "Not exactly. I need to talk to you."

He raised a brow, then stepped aside. "Please, come in."

The doorway was wide, and she was able to avoid brushing past him too closely. Still, his strong presence radiated toward her as she passed by, trying to draw her in again. She sensed his maleness, visceral and wholly innate. Known to him but unseen to her own eyes.

Vanessa was grateful when he closed the door behind him.

The fourth floor seemed empty and, to her knowledge, held only Gregory's office. She knew Prentice wouldn't budge from his chair unless he had to go "make water," she thought disgustedly.

It appeared the two of them were alone, and that was a good thing. She wanted the conversation she was about to have to be completely private.

"I'm surprised you're still here. It is Friday night, you know."

He gestured to a chair in front of his desk. "Contrary to popular belief, being a mayor is a twenty-four-hour job."

She sat down on the edge and placed her hands on her knees to stop them from trembling.

Her eyes tracked him as he walked from the door to the other side of his desk. And when he got there, he stopped abruptly and seemed to be contemplating whether or not he should sit down.

She forced herself to keep her eyes on his face, instead of letting them wander down to his powerful thighs. Both were distracting.

"Oh, how so?"

"As you know, Bay Point is a small town. We don't have a lot of resources. I have to ensure the enforcement of city ordinances, provide leadership to the community and handle other duties."

"That's quite a list, Mayor. Do you like your job?"

His slow grin sent a delicious thrill through her body. "It keeps me busy. And out of trouble."

His wooden chair squeaked loudly as he sat down, but he didn't seem to notice. "What about you? Late day at the flower shop?"

Vanessa nodded. "I had deliveries in the morning, but this afternoon was slow until just as I was about to close."

He folded his hands behind his head and leaned back against the chair. "What happened?"

She smiled at the memory. "Two customers came in at almost the same time. One was a nervous teen going on his first date. The other was a guilt-torn husband who somehow forgot his wife's birthday."

Gregory winced. "Two tough scenarios. I'm glad I've only been in one of those."

"Oh? You remember your first date?"

He straightened and laughed. "Only that it was a disaster. I was a nervous wreck."

Vanessa had attended Bay Point High School, while Gregory had gone to an expensive private school. Back then she rarely saw him, but she did recall that he'd been really skinny. Now he was so muscular and full of confidence it was hard to imagine that he was once an awkward adolescent struggling to become a man.

"I wouldn't peg you as being nervous about anything."

Something changed in his voice. It wasn't regret—rather something akin to hope.

"There's a lot you don't know about me, Vanessa." He paused. "But there's something I know about you."

Vanessa felt the blood drain from her face. Had her father told him the real reason she'd come back to Bay Point? If he had, she might as well just get up and walk out the door. Like a petal torn from a flower, what she had lost could not be replaced.

She tightened her grip on her knees. "What's that?"

He inched closer to his desk. "That you're great with customers."

His statement was so deliberate and matter-of-fact, so completely opposite to the suspicion that her mind had induced, that she found it difficult not to sink back against her chair in relief.

"I just treat them the way I expect to be treated— with kindness, dignity and respect."

"Your customers aren't perfect, so you have to be," he said.

Oh, if he only knew.

In her daily work, her efforts brought joy to some, pain or indifference to others. Surrounded by perfect beauty and radiant color all day, inhaling the fragrant essence and earthiness of life that had been created millions of years ago, she was constantly reminded of her fallibility and her blessings. The struggle to remember to be thankful was real.

Vanessa shrugged. "I'm not infallible, Mayor. I make mistakes. I just try not to make them twice."

Gregory looked at her intently and her stomach fluttered wildly, a sign of attraction that she viewed as a warning. She rubbed at her wrist nervously.

"Did you get hurt today?"

The concern in his voice surprised her. "Not really. Just a little cramp."

He smiled. "I'm glad to hear it. I didn't think floral arranging was a dangerous profession."

His tone was respectful rather than jeering, and she wondered what he would do if she really were hurt. Would he cradle her in his strong arms? His warm hazel eyes were the kind she could easily get lost in under the right conditions.

Vanessa took a deep breath. "No more dangerous than agreeing to be your campaign manager," she blurted out.

She'd wanted to ease into the conversation, not make it sound as if she were overly excited to work with him. This time she was in control, not the other way around. This time she wouldn't allow herself to be hurt.

The smile left his face, but it was back seconds later, wide with pleasure, as if he'd just won the biggest stuffed animal at the county fair.

He leaned forward and cupped his ear. "Say again? Did you just agree to be my—"

"Campaign manager," she replied with a stern nod.

He paused again, as if he still couldn't believe what he was hearing, and Vanessa got a glimpse of that gangly adolescent boy who had just scored his first date.

"That's great!" he exclaimed.

Vanessa held back a smile as she watched him nearly leap out of his chair, which creaked in response like old bedsprings. He rounded the desk and stuck out his hand. But instead of shaking it, she lifted her index finger.

"But there's one condition."

He dropped his hand, and his smile faltered just a bit. "Name it."

She stood up. "You have to promise not to tear down the carousel."

Gregory frowned. "I can't promise that, Vanessa."

Her stomach dropped in fear, but she wasn't going to stop now.

"Wait. Just hear me out. If I can find a way to fix it up, at no cost to the city, then would you at least consider leaving it alone?"

Gregory averted his eyes. When they returned to her face moments later, still warm, still happy, Vanessa recognized the barest hint of pain in them.

"I'll consider it," he said firmly.

He started to speak again, but she held up her index finger once more to stop him.

"And," she continued, "Mayor, you have to agree to hear the opinions of the local businesses about the redevelopment plan, because we—none of us—had the opportunity to voice them during the discussion and planning stages."

There was no hesitation this time. "Deal."

He leaned against the desk in such a relaxed manner that it was easy to imagine him doing the same motion in her kitchen on a Saturday morning, except in that instance, he'd be shirtless and dressed in only his underwear. Or maybe just his black fedora. Or perhaps nothing at all.

Her face flushed hot, and she dismissed the thought. That would never happen, not if she wanted to maintain control.

Almost there.

Gregory started to extend his hand again and abruptly paused. "Wait a second. That's two conditions, isn't it?"

"I guess it is," she said with a smile. "Let's make it an uneven three."

He linked his hands together in front of his body. "You're a demanding woman, you know that?" Rather than sounding cross, his tone was akin to admiration. "What is it?"

Vanessa took a deep breath. "Total transparency," she said curtly. "You have to be totally honest with me about all aspects of the redevelopment project."

He reared back, as if offended. "Agreed. But what makes you think I haven't been honest thus far?"

She stood her ground. "As I told you yesterday, the other store owners felt blindsided by the announcement. A lot of them, including me, felt that you could have talked to us beforehand."

"Believe me, Vanessa. I had every intention of doing so, but the news was released before I had a chance."

"What? How could that happen? Don't you have any control over your public relations efforts?"

He grimaced. "Now do you see why I need a campaign manager?"

"What about your assistant?"

"Mariella?" He shook his head. "She's responsible for documenting the feedback we receive from the public through phone calls, emails and the city's website, scheduling meetings or other administrative duties. She's not a PR person."

"Then who released the information without your approval? Over the past several weeks, there have been rumors flying around town, but nothing specific."

Gregory hesitated, and Vanessa frowned. "I wasn't kidding, Mayor. If you want me to help you sell the merits of the redevelopment plan, I have to be privy to all the details."

"George Stodwell," he said grimly.

"Stodwell? Why?"

Vanessa was barely able to keep her extreme dislike of the man out of her voice.

George Stodwell was considered to be the most hated man in Bay Point, but she had no idea how Gregory felt about the transplanted New Yorker. She and everyone else in town wished he'd hightail it back to the Big Apple. But year after year, Stodwell stayed. Getting fatter, richer and lazier. It was rumored that the man didn't even shave himself. He paid someone to do it every morning.

"Even before I was in office, the former mayor started talking about redeveloping downtown Bay Point. Stodwell has been on the planning commission all along. As a property owner, he has a vested interest in garnering support for this project and seeing it completed as quickly as possible. He simply called in a favor over at the paper, and ba-da-bing, front-page news."

Vanessa made a face, no longer willing to hold back her opinion. "He's no better than a New York City slumlord. I can't tell you how many repairs he's promised to make in my apartment, let alone my shop, that he's never completed. Stodwell's lack of response to all of his tenants over the past several months is infuriating."

He frowned, his eyes crinkling at the edges. "Look, I'll talk to him, okay? Maybe there's a good reason why he hasn't been responsive."

"Yeah, like the fact that he doesn't care about his tenants or Bay Point?"

Vanessa rolled her eyes and spotted a gaping hole in the corner of one ceiling tile. The wood slats from the subfloor above were visible. It was clear that even the mayor's office needed repairs.

Gregory was probably used to having the best of everything. She wondered how he dealt with being in less-than-luxurious working conditions.

She walked over and pointed at the hole. "Looks like you've got some pretty serious repair projects of your own."

Gregory joined her in the corner of the room. His waist was trim, and the contour of his backside underneath his gray pants gave her an unexpected thrill.

He clasped his hands on his hips, looked up at the ceiling and frowned. "That's been there since before I was voted into office. The only improvements I've authorized to be made were necessary ones, like keeping the air-conditioning system in good working order, but all of that is about to change."

"The new municipal complex. It's also part of the redevelopment plan, isn't that right?"

"Yes." He nodded and faced her. "City hall hasn't had a major renovation since it was built in 1920. In today's dollars, the cost to fix everything that needs to be done is too high."

His stance was businesslike. He stood close enough that she could reach out and touch him now, but he still wasn't encroaching on her personal space.

She appreciated his professionalism. Because she could sense within herself, the way the hairs on her arms started to prickle, that if he took just one step closer, that if she even brushed against the fabric of his crisp white shirt, she would have a difficult time breathing.

"It's cheaper to demolish and start over," Vanessa concluded.

Gregory nodded. "Right. That's why the carousel is being torn down. It simply doesn't work with the blueprints that our architect has presented."

Vanessa frowned at his comment, as it reminded her that saving the carousel wasn't going to be easy, especially if it wasn't even going to be part of the new municipal center.

"When I get the carousel fixed, you'll just have to tell your architect to draw up some new plans."

Gregory stared at her as if she'd just made the most outlandish and impossible request ever. And maybe she had. But it was easier to tear up a blueprint than to tear down a structure that had made a positive impact on so many people and families in Bay Point.

"I know how you feel about the carousel, but it's not that simple."

He walked over to the desk again. Vanessa followed, trying to keep the anger from creeping into her voice at his patronizing comment. "With all due respect, Mayor, you don't know how I feel about the carousel or anything else, for that matter, and I'd like to keep it that way."

The wedge of a shadow crossed Gregory's face, and Vanessa immediately regretted her terse reaction.

"Transparency doesn't apply to you, only to me? That's fine," he agreed, though his tone held a note of disappointment that Vanessa found strangely endearing.

"However, maybe someday you'll feel comfortable telling me why the carousel is so important to you."

"Why? Will doing so make it easier to change your mind about tearing it down?" she demanded, trying not to sound hopeful.

Although Gregory seemed like a decent man, he was still a politician. He was probably used to saying anything to anyone, if it got him what he wanted.

"No," Gregory admitted, to Vanessa's relief. "But at least I'll have a peek into what lies beneath that tough-girl act you seem to put on whenever we're in the same room together."

Without realizing it, she put one hand on her hip. "Tough-girl act?"

"Yeah," he said, stepping closer. "Your lips. They purse together the same way they used to when we played together as kids. When I would get you dirty."

"What are you talking about?"

Before she knew what was happening, he reached out and casually put the tip of his finger against her mouth. It felt like a rod of fire against her flesh, as he softly rolled it from the center of her lips to each corner and back to center. Her flesh immediately softened, and the core of her being flashed white-hot with desire.

"That's better."

He stepped away, but she still felt the hot ghost of the pressure of his finger. There was nothing illicit about his statement or his smile, only a flash of amusement.

When she involuntarily touched her hand to her mouth, she wanted to kick herself. He shouldn't have touched her, but he didn't seem to notice anything was wrong. It was obvious by the look on his face that whatever she had felt at that moment was not shared by him.

"We played together one time. One time," she repeated. "How can you remember that?"

"Oh, I remember."

She crossed her arms. Her nipples were hard. She could feel them beneath her padded bra. Though she didn't think Gregory could see them, this time she didn't want to take any chances.

So she walked away and stood in front of a pencil-

and-ink drawing of Bay Point that was hanging on Gregory's wall. But before she had the chance to really study it, she turned around quickly.

"Wait a second. You were the one who hated to get muddy, not me."

He laughed. "You're right. I'm surprised you remembered."

"I am, too," she admitted. "To be honest, I actually don't recall too much about that day."

Gregory stepped toward her and she held her breath, surprised at how much she wanted him to touch her lips again. "Then you probably forgot that I hated to see you go?"

"Why? Our mothers forced us to play together."

"I didn't need to be forced, Vanessa. I *wanted* to play with you. Even though we went to different schools, I'd seen you and your family around town from time to time. Your parents seemed really cool."

Vanessa thought for a moment. Her mom, Jewel, was a stay-at-home mom and an activist. Her father, Ned, was a respected physician and head of emergency at Bay Point Community Hospital. They'd been married over thirty years, had raised her and her brother and were still very much in love.

"Yeah. They still are, but where are you going with this, Mayor?"

"It sounds like you've agreed to be my campaign manager, and I'm really happy about that, but I must admit I'm a little curious as to why the sudden change of heart. Did your mom force you into it, like the playdate we had all those years ago, as part of her latest cause?"

Vanessa shook her head. "No. She doesn't even know I'm here. I just care about Bay Point too much to let it die. This is my hometown, and I'm going to do everything in my power to keep it thriving."

"It's my hometown, too, Vanessa. And despite what you, Jacob Billingsly and everyone else in town might think right now, I want to ensure that Bay Point remains a wonderful and safe place to live."

She desperately wanted to believe him, believe that he really cared about the town. Still, she had her doubts.

After all, she'd worked with plenty of politicians who had covered up their true feelings to gain popularity and votes. But if she was going to be his campaign manager, she needed to at least try to lay aside her doubts. Otherwise, she would never gain his trust, which was the first step to changing his mind about the carousel.

She held out her hand. It was now or never. "It's getting late. If you're in agreement with all of my requests, I'm looking forward to helping you achieve that goal."

His hand was warm in hers, and when he released his respectful grip, she felt a sense of cold and loss.

"So it's official." At her nod, he clasped both of his hands together. "I can't wait to hear your ideas."

"I've already got one."

He raised a brow. "Let's hear it."

"I think we should have a town hall meeting. Get everyone in one room so you can explain the redevelopment plan and allow people to come forward in a public forum with questions and complaints and suggestions. I will help you craft the messaging so it's positive and impactful to help you further gain support for the project."

Gregory nodded. "I like it. And what's our plan of attack against Billingsly?"

"That's going to require a little more thought on my part. We're going to need a sound strategy."

"Fine. How much time do you need?"

"Only a few days. I'll call you to set up a time to meet."

"Or we could have a working dinner. I know this great little spot. I know you have a shop to run, and I don't want to interfere with the operation of your business in any way."

Vanessa shook her head. "Evenings are when I'm going to be doing most of the work on the campaign. I think we should just meet in your office sometime next week, first thing in the morning. I'll bring the coffee."

He didn't seem at all disappointed by her refusal to have dinner with him.

"Of course. Don't worry. I've already reserved some money out of my campaign budget to pay you."

Vanessa shook her head. "That's not necessary, Mayor. I'm volunteering my time, for the good of Bay Point."

He softened his voice, and there was a level of tenderness that she could not ignore but would never be able to replicate perfectly in her head. He accompanied her to the door. "Thank you, Vanessa. I really appreciate this."

"Don't thank me until you win the election."

As she walked down the hall to the elevator, her heart was bursting with excitement. There was still time to save the carousel. Now all she had to do was come up with a plan.

Chapter 6

Vanessa eased her yellow convertible under a cluster of palm trees, stopped and switched off the ignition. She turned in her seat and glanced around, a little uneasily. About a mile back, she'd passed a hand-written sign with slanted block letters: *PRIVATE. NO TRESPASSING.*

Earlier that morning, Gregory had emailed her that this was the way to the Langston private beach, so she supposed she was in the right place. She stepped out of the car and didn't bother to lock it.

A wooden platform was a few feet away, with stairs leading down a steep cliff to the beach. The Pacific Ocean beckoned with a combination of hope and recklessness. From a distance, though, the water appeared calm, but she could still hear the waves softly crashing onto the shore.

The sun was on its way down to meet the horizon. Vanessa had the odd sense that it was waiting for something to complete its journey. She held her breath, mesmerized by the scene for a moment. Perhaps it was waiting for her. But of course, that was impossible, and the thought was a little crazy.

Kinda like meeting Gregory. On a private beach. With no one else in sight.

Reckless.

Tomorrow was the town hall meeting. They both knew that how Gregory handled it could make or break his election to a second term. Vanessa had agreed to meet him at the beach partly because it was more relaxed than his office. The other reason lay deep within her heart, yet she wasn't ready to admit it yet.

Hope.

Vanessa leaned over the passenger side, slanted the rearview mirror toward her and frowned. Her hair was tousled from the open-air drive, and she'd forgotten her hat at the shop. She loved her car, but her hair didn't, so she smoothed it down as best as she could and then walked slowly to the platform.

The stairs were weathered gray. They were sandy and the wood splintered in some places, but they were solidly anchored to the side of the cliff. Still, she held on to the rail and kept her eyes focused on making it down to the beach safely. It was only a few minutes until she reached the bottom.

She slipped off her sandals. Lifting her head, she spotted a man lying on the beach, just outside of a stony nook in the cliff a few hundred feet away. The black fedora canted over his face left no question that it was Gregory.

Vanessa took a few steps forward. He appeared to be sunbathing, and Vanessa couldn't help but be awkwardly disappointed that his shirt was on. But why wouldn't it be? This was a business meeting, not a personal peep show.

She had a deep admiration for Gregory and all that he had accomplished thus far in his career. Other than that, she wasn't sure what she felt about him. Or how he felt about her.

Since they'd started working together, he'd displayed no obvious signs of attraction, and she'd taken extra precautions to do the same, maintaining interested yet cool eye contact when he was speaking to her and a professional distance when they were sitting in his office.

But now, watching him from a short distance away, in spite of their differing opinions on the redevelopment plan, she would have given anything to see the body that was at the core of his power. Without the trappings of politics. Or clothes. The one that made him a man.

Tiptoeing closer, she realized that Gregory was dozing. Half under the hat, his eyes were closed. His chest rose and fell under his creamy linen shirt, and she could see a few dots of perspiration at the base of his neck. The breeze had curled back the bottom right edge of his shirt, revealing just a hint of his rock-solid abs. Her mind rolled through dangerous territory as her eyes traced down his black surf shorts and muscular calves.

She kicked sand on his bare feet. "Sleeping on the job, Mayor?"

He awoke with a start and cracked open both eyes. "Wh-at?"

Vanessa crossed her arms around her chest and hid a smile.

Gregory looked pretty cute when he was startled. This made it impossible to be mad at him. Still, she ignored his yawn and gave him the best evil eye she could muster.

"We've got a big day tomorrow. Shouldn't you be going over your notes instead of resting?"

He palmed his hat and eased it back on top of his head. The lower half of his face had the barest hint of brown-black stubble. He squinted up at her, sleepy eyed.

"Power naps are a good thing."

"So is regular practice," she reminded him.

Gregory propped himself up by his elbows, and she was treated to a glimpse of the tight and curly black hair on his chest. "That's why I asked you to come down here. To help me go over things."

She scanned the sand around him. It was empty, with nary a flip-flop. "So where's your speech?"

Now sitting cross-legged, Gregory glanced up at her and she trained her eyes on him, even though his lap looked like a good place for her to nestle in and get absolutely nothing done.

"I didn't bring it," he replied. A hint of grogginess in his voice gave it a rugged sound. "I figured that if I don't know what I'm going to say by now, I might as well call off the town meeting."

Vanessa gasped. "You can't cancel. We've worked too hard, and the people of Bay Point need answers."

Gregory got to his feet. "Sure I can, and do you know why? Because even after all of our meetings, I still get the sense that you don't have any confidence in me."

His eyes darkened, not in accusation but in challenge. "Do you?"

Vanessa's eyes widened at his question, which seemed more personal than professional.

Her job was to ensure that the things he said in the community overall, but especially about the redevelopment plan, would help to pave the way to his being reelected to a second term. Why would he care about what she thought about him personally?

Without looking at her, Gregory started to brush the sand from his clothes. His actions gave her a chance to think about her response, but they were also a little disquieting.

Earlier she'd changed from her shop uniform into

a white eyelet sundress so she could feel the heat on her arms and the wind skating along her skin as she drove. Looking good for the mayor hadn't even crossed her mind.

But something in the haphazard way he was sweeping the sand from his clothes made her suddenly yearn for him to notice her. Not like a road sign or those digital billboards that were like watching television at sixty-five miles per hour. But more like the intricate ridges of a seashell, the uniqueness of a fingerprint or the mystery of a smile.

"Of course I do," she finally managed. "Or else I wouldn't be here. What kind of campaign manager doesn't have confidence in her leader?"

Gregory looked up and smiled, a trace of relief on his face. "Good, because without you, I'm sunk. You know what they say—behind every good man—"

"Is a woman who makes sure he doesn't trip and fall on his ass," she finished.

He laughed, full on from the stomach, and strangely, it felt warmer than the sand beneath her feet.

Gregory started to walk toward the coastline. "Come on. I've got to get this sand off my hands."

She dropped her sandals and followed him. "You know, Mayor, even if I didn't have a speck of confidence in you, you'd still be just fine without me."

He looked back over his shoulder at her. For the first time, she was struck by the strong angle of his jaw. It seemed almost naked now, without the underscore of his collared dress shirt.

He stopped in his tracks, and she nearly ran into him. "Don't tell me that you're thinking about quitting on me."

"Not at all," she assured him, taking a step back. "But even if I did, you'd be okay."

Gregory gave her a quizzical look and kept moving. "I wouldn't be doing my first-ever town hall meeting, that's for sure."

She followed and soon they reached the edge of the shore. She stood close by as Gregory went a little farther, then bent down and wiggled his hands in the ocean water. The waves rushed over his bare feet and back out to sea.

"And that's a bad thing?" she asked, digging her toes into the wet sand.

"No," he said, righting himself and shaking his hands to the side.

She squealed and jumped back a little, trying to avoid the droplets of water from his hands.

"Sorry. I didn't mean to get you wet."

"It's okay. I won't melt."

The first three buttons of his linen shirt were undone, and it was hard not to stare at the muscular swell of his chest beneath the thin material. She could get used to seeing him like this. So playfully natural. Free from the stuffy suit and tie he normally wore, although he looked delicious in those, too.

"I must admit—" Gregory's voice dipped low, as if he were afraid someone would hear what he was going to say, and he wiped his hands dry on his shorts "—I'm a little nervous about tomorrow."

A warning bell sounded in her head, the type that could strike a death knell to Gregory's election campaign.

"What are you talking about, Mayor? You've got this," she assured him. "Besides, I have confidence in you."

"I know that now."

She thought Gregory's concerns were appeased when he treated her to a half smile, but when it quickly flattened to a wistful line, she knew there was something wrong.

Vanessa knew that if Jacob Billingsly got even a whiff that Mayor Langston wasn't completely comfortable and confident with the town hall forum, he would use it to gain an advantage in the election race. She couldn't allow that to happen.

Despite their differing opinions, she'd spent enough time with Gregory that she did not want to see him lose. Not because she was his campaign manager, and certainly not because she was attracted to him. But simply because Jacob Billingsly was a horrible and sneaky man.

Gregory stuck his hands in his front pockets. "When I was practicing law full-time, I had no problem in front of the jury. Getting twelve people to see my point was easy, for the most part." He sighed heavily. "But now I have to convince an entire town."

"Not so easy," Vanessa admitted, not to bolster him up, but because what he said was true.

He nodded and looked over toward the horizon, giving her another glimpse at the strong line of his jaw. "The redevelopment plan could be the most successful building project that Bay Point has experienced since it was established as a town back in the early 1900s."

"But it also has the potential to be a huge failure," she added.

She'd said as much to him when he'd first asked her to be his campaign manager, though not as nicely. It occurred to her now that her once-negative view of the plan was slowly morphing into something else. Not overt acceptance. She didn't know if she would *ever* get to that point. Though it helped that she was doing her part in preserving the historical character of the town by trying to save the carousel.

Gregory turned back, looped his hands together and brought them over his head. She watched the muscles of his arms lengthen as he stretched them up toward the purple-and-pink-streaked sky.

The tiny dark buds of his nipples were clearly evident through the thin material of his shirt. An odd side effect of stretching, she wondered, or was it something else?

She crossed her legs at the ankles and felt her insides twinge with pleasure at the visual treat he'd unconsciously given her.

Gregory let his arms fall to the sides of his body.

"The chance that this whole plan could fail. That's what worries me. Keeps me up at night."

He paused and stepped closer to her. "Among other things."

Vanessa's breath hitched in her throat. "Like what?"

He wasn't standing close enough to her that if anyone happened to see them, they would suspect something was going on. Because nothing was going on, she reminded herself. Still, her face grew hot and her throat constricted slightly at being that much nearer to him.

Suddenly, Gregory crouched down. His surf shorts were like a second skin against his backside.

He picked up a small flat rock from the shore and fingered it, looking out somewhere in the distance.

"As you already know, before I was a mayor, I was a lawyer. And before that—"

"You were a kid making mud patties," she teased playfully.

She slid her feet lightly across the sand to be closer to him, not caring that her blue-painted toenails were getting ruined.

No one was around.

No one was watching.

She stopped when her thighs were perpendicular to his right shoulder.

Gregory's eyes raked up her bare skin and, whether he meant to or not, left her wanting more.

He grinned up at her. "That, too, but I also wanted to be an architect."

A light breeze rustled her dress. Gregory was close enough that he could potentially see up her skirt. She flattened her palms against her thighs to keep the material down.

"Somehow I can't imagine you sitting at a drafting table with a bunch of blueprints stuffed under your armpit. Why didn't you?"

He stood up and, with a quick flick of his wrist, tossed the rock into the ocean, so far that Vanessa couldn't even see where it landed.

"A sense of obligation," Gregory said, turning to her almost sheepishly. "To my family, but mostly to my dad."

Obligation. Vanessa shuddered inwardly. She understood all too well what that word meant.

"My family isn't nearly as wealthy as yours, and my father isn't nearly as well-known in California as yours, but I can understand how hard it is to be the child of parents who've accomplished a lot in their lives."

Gregory blew out a breath. "I knew you'd get it. Your father is a gem. I don't know what the town would do without him. The improvements he's made in patient care at Bay Point Community Hospital deserve a lot more attention than they've been receiving."

"He prefers to stay in the background."

Gregory touched the brim of his hat, then picked

up another small rock and tossed it into the ocean. It skipped on the waves and sunk out of sight.

"Like his daughter?"

Vanessa thought a moment, then nodded. "Yes. My mom is always the one on the front lines of the causes she champions. She's the one picketing, holding up the most accusatory signs, confronting the issues with facts, not feelings."

"And you?"

She tilted her head. "What do you think?"

"Hmm...let's see." Gregory put his hands behind his back, and he looked at her intensely, as if he was studying her. "Quiet, determined, focused."

She made a face. "Ugh. You make me sound so boring."

He unclasped his hands and laughed. "No, just stable. And that's good."

Gregory's brow crinkled into pensive lines, and he looked troubled. "As for me, sometimes I wonder if I should just move on. Go back to working in my father's law firm."

Vanessa's heart beat faster. "Don't you like being mayor?"

Gregory nodded, but the movement was hesitant. "It's just that I wonder what would have happened if I'd stood up to my father all those years back and just been an architect."

"You wouldn't be standing here on the beach with me," she teased.

"Then I made the right decision." Gregory gazed

into her eyes, and she saw that he was telling the truth. "You want me to be transparent with you, correct?"

"Well, that *was* part of the deal," she answered, hoping she didn't sound smug.

"This redevelopment project? I have my own selfish purposes."

Vanessa stared at him, wide-eyed and stunned. Since she'd worked with politicians before, her mind went immediately south to kickbacks, money exchanging hands in back alleys, offshore wire transfers and other headline-news-inducing, career-destroying criminal acts.

Gregory took a step back. "The look on your face could sway a jury. Hold up. It's not what you think." He folded his arms. "It's been a childhood dream of mine. To make something old new again. I may never be an architect, but I can be a part of building something great. A new legacy. Too bad no one in Bay Point seems to want that but me."

Vanessa felt her insides deflate with relief, a sign of all the negative things she'd thought Gregory could be involved in, but thankfully, he was not. Since she'd started working with him, she constantly had to remind herself that not all politicians were dirty and underhanded.

"That's why we're having the town hall meeting. To convince them that this is the right thing to do."

"Do you really believe that?"

His wish for a "new" downtown Bay Point was

valid, but so was her wish for the carousel to remain unscathed at the town's center, and this wasn't the time to argue with him about it.

"It doesn't matter what I believe. It's what the people of Bay Point, the people you serve, believe. And tomorrow is our chance to get a pulse from the community on the redevelopment issue."

Gregory nodded. "You're right. But it doesn't help our cause that Billingsly is feeding the people lies. I mean, he's claiming that the construction materials are going to cause environmental problems. We haven't even selected a supplier yet!"

"I agree. We both know all he's doing is blowing smoke. He has no basis for his outrageous claims."

Gregory shoved his hands in his pockets again. "You and I know that. But what if people start listening to him?"

"Then we'll just have to shout a little louder." She reached over and touched his arm. "So no one can hear him."

He grinned, withdrew his hands from his pockets. "That's what I like about you. You're so level-headed."

He held his arms open, and for a split second, Vanessa thought he was going to hug her. But instead he bent down and scooped up some dry sand.

"Do me a favor—cup your hands for me."

"What?" she asked. "Why?"

"Don't ask any questions. Just do it. Cup your hands together as tightly as you can."

Gregory gently placed the sand into her palm.

Vanessa tried to keep it in, but eventually the tiny granules slipped away and fell back on the beach.

"See how the sand cannot be imprisoned," Gregory said, his voice hushed. "No matter what you do or how hard you try to hold on to it, it always finds a way to escape. To have its freedom."

In moments, all the sand was gone.

"Is that what you want to do, Gregory? Escape?"

"Sometimes…" His voice trailed off. "Don't you?"

Before she could answer, the wind suddenly picked up, and Gregory's hat blew off his head.

Without thinking, Vanessa turned and ran into the water. She bent down to retrieve Gregory's hat from where it was floating and almost got walloped upright by one swell of waves.

He waded in after her, grabbed her hand and helped her out. "Thanks," he said when they were back onshore.

He released her hand slowly. "You didn't have to do that."

She handed him his hat. Their wet fingers slid together again.

"I didn't want it to go into the ocean and have a shark or whale swallow it up."

The wind kicked up again, and by the goose bumps and chill on her skin, she knew that her dress was wet.

She didn't dare look down, but she knew that her bra was sheer, and now her dress was even sheerer and clinging to her body. She'd been so intent on getting his hat that she hadn't even noticed.

"I'm levelheaded, remember?" Vanessa said, appreciating that he was trying hard not to stare.

The water swirled around their feet, and they both jumped back.

Gregory slapped his hat against his muscular thighs to get the water out, then put it back on his head. "Tide's coming in."

"Y-yeah," she stammered. "I've got to get back. Early deliveries at the hospital in the morning." Though it was the truth, in her ears the words somehow sounded like an excuse.

They stared at each other a moment, and she shifted her feet and awkwardly folded her arms across her chest.

"What about you, Mayor? Are you headed home?"

He lifted his chin toward the cliff. "Nah, I'm going to walk over to my mom and dad's. It's only a mile or so down the beach."

She found her sandals and picked them up, glad for something to hold on to. Then she felt his toe touch hers.

"Tell you what. Wear a dress like that tomorrow night, and no one will be listening to me."

Vanessa turned and smiled, and the heat on her back as she walked away wasn't from the rays of the sun.

Chapter 7

Last night on the beach, Gregory had a revelation.

Perhaps it was seeing Vanessa somewhere other than the flower shop or in his office. Or maybe because for the first time they'd had some privacy, just the two of them.

But all of a sudden he knew. Vanessa Hamilton was a woman who deserved someone special, someone who would cherish her, more than all night long.

A man like him? Maybe.

He fingered the square edges of his gold cuff links as he listened to Vanessa run through the talking points again. She insisted on going over them again, even though he knew them backward and forward.

It was the tone of her voice that he couldn't quite capture. It was lush yet subdued, like the first days of summer. Hearing her now invoked a swell of carnal yearning, and he turned away abruptly to regain control.

Vanessa stopped talking midsentence. "Was it something I said?"

Her voice was a mixture of innocence and concern, neither forced. She seemed genuine, her beauty natural. He didn't have to hide with her, but he did anyway. It was easier that way.

Gregory took a deep breath. A bad idea.

He'd forgotten how stale and musty the air was in the meeting room. Located in the basement of city hall, it also doubled as a community theater. There was a small raised stage, a worn red velvet curtain and plenty of bad musicals in its long history.

"N-no," he stammered, trying not to cough. "I thought I was going to sneeze. That's all."

Vanessa sniffed lightly. "It is kind of dank down here."

Gregory waited a beat, until he was sure his body had settled down, and faced her. "Just another reason why Bay Point needs a new city hall."

"Should I add it to the talking points?"

He shook his head. "No. I don't want to give people another reason why they should hate the redevelopment plan."

She nodded. "For once, I have to agree with you."

Gregory chuckled. "Bet you never thought that would happen."

"What do you mean?"

"That we would work as a team."

His eyes drifted to hers, a little deeper than they probably should have, but they were alone. It was easy to look at her, even easier to want her. What was more difficult was figuring out how to stop wanting her.

Vanessa suddenly sneezed. She seemed completely unaware of how she affected him.

"Bless you," he said, and they both laughed.

"I hope you're not allergic to me," he joked.

Vanessa didn't answer, her smile disappearing, replaced by a glimmer in her eyes as if she was trying to remember something, or maybe forget.

They both paused and listened to the past, present and future all colliding in the murmur of the crowd.

"Sounds like there are a lot of people out there."

Vanessa parted the curtain a little. Next to the swath of red velvet, her hands seemed unusually small. She wore no rings. Still, she was like a gypsy, slowly drawing him into her world, casting her spell on him.

"It's standing room only. Prentice is busy setting up some extra chairs."

He groaned softly and took a step closer to her. "For once, I wish he would get busy napping."

Vanessa released the curtain. "He's good at that, isn't he?" She laughed quietly. "But don't worry. The more people, the better."

Gregory frowned. "You're not the one who has to face them."

He never got this nervous before speaking, but he didn't have time to ponder if it was the crowd or the woman standing next to him who was at fault. The meeting was going to start in less than five minutes.

He swore inwardly, then muttered, "The butterflies are working overtime tonight."

"Hey. An engaged community is a good thing," Vanessa reminded him, her soft voice almost a whisper.

"I know," he replied, peeking through a small opening in the curtain. "I just didn't expect there to be so many folks here."

"Don't worry, Mayor. You are well prepared."

He felt her hand gently tug on his arm. "Scratch that. *We* are well prepared."

Gregory stepped back and smiled, his anxiety ebbing away at her touch. She said "we" so firmly and full of confidence, with just a touch of possessiveness, as if they were partners on some kind of important quest.

Unbeknownst to Vanessa, he'd already discovered something fascinating. She had the ability to turn his body rock hard and his mind into mush, all at the same time. No other woman had been able to command his attention as she had done.

Vanessa cleared her throat and tapped one finger on her lips. She took a step back and considered him intently. He felt like squirming but didn't and wished she would look at him with more interest than as though she were viewing a sliver of a specimen under a microscope.

She paused and shook her head. "There's just one little thing we need to change."

His heart plummeted, his anxiety returning full tilt. Last-minute changes were never on his agenda.

She seemed to float toward him, clad in a light gray dress, professional yet devastatingly elegant. He found himself holding his breath, but when she stood in front of him, somehow he managed to speak.

"What is it?"

Butterflies back on the job fluttered madly in his stomach. He knew that this time it wasn't the crowd that was causing his nerves to tailspin; it was Vanessa.

She leaned in close and whispered, "Your tie. It's all wrong."

"Really, how can you tell?" he whispered back, bringing both hands to his neck.

"The knot isn't exactly perfect," she replied, matching his whisper. "I'm a florist, remember? I've tied hundreds of knots over the years."

Gregory hitched an index finger to remove his tie and start over. "Guess I broke the first rule of politics—presentation is everything."

"Oh yeah? What's the second rule?" she asked.

He caught a whiff of her perfume. It was subtle, a flowery scent, something like lilacs and vanilla. And it was completely intoxicating.

She didn't seem to notice when he bent a little

closer, his mouth near her ear. So close he could have licked her lobe. God, how he wanted to. For once, he was thankful that there were hundreds of people just beyond the velvet curtain.

"That's the joke. There are no rules in politics," he whispered.

Vanessa laughed quietly, as if she understood exactly what he meant.

Gregory knew she'd worked for other political leaders when she was living in Los Angeles. What he didn't know was why she'd returned home. Not that he wanted to pry, really—she was here right now, standing before him. For now, that was all that mattered.

Vanessa's fingers, slender and cool, touched his hands.

"Let me do it," she instructed.

At six feet tall, he towered over most women, but Vanessa didn't have to stretch far to reach him.

He stood straight, like a schoolboy. All he could hear was the gentle sliding of his tie being expertly undone in her hands.

Gregory had never been this close to her before. In his office, having coffee at Ruby's, even on the beach, they'd always maintained a respectful distance.

Now all he wanted to do was get even closer.

She had a tiny mole on the outside corner of one eyebrow. Her skin was clear and smooth, her makeup expertly applied but not heavy. Her berry-colored lips pursed with concentration as her hands ministered to him.

When she finished, she smoothed some dust from his shoulders and smiled. He didn't need a mirror to know that he looked good. He could see it in the glow of her eyes, and her appreciation of him chased the remaining butterflies in his stomach away.

"I guess I'm not one of those guys who can tie a tie without looking in a mirror." *Or without a beautiful woman assisting me.*

If he told her that, would she believe him, or would she dismiss his words as easily as he could kiss her right now?

Gregory knew he couldn't take the chance. Whatever his feelings, he was going to keep them inside. Knotted up as perfectly as his tie.

He checked his watch. "Showtime. You ready?"

Vanessa nodded, parted the curtain again and stepped up to the podium, while he remained backstage. He rolled his shoulders back to ease the tension in them while she briefly explained the format of the meeting to the audience. When she introduced him, he stepped onstage.

The healthy applause and the scent of Vanessa's floral perfume lingering in the air comforted him as he headed to the podium.

He adjusted the mike and began. "Thank you all for your time this evening. Our town is at a critical juncture in its history. Scores of our friends and neighbors have moved due to lack of employment opportunities. Businesses have shut down or moved out of the area."

Gregory paused and looked around the room. Faces he recognized and those he didn't were peering at him.

"But we are not alone."

His voice caught in his throat, suppressing a burst of emotion, but he quickly recovered. "Small towns and cities across America are experiencing the exact same challenges. It is revitalizing those areas that are central to life in towns such as ours that has resulted in the renaissance of Main Streets throughout our country."

Gregory smiled easily. "My redevelopment plan creates opportunities for tourists to stay, shop and dine. Plus, it will also attract new residents to rent or buy properties."

He gripped his hands on the dark worn wood of the podium. Although Vanessa was standing on the far right of the stage, he could still sense her presence, renewing his vigor.

"Four years ago, when you voted me into this office, I promised to do everything I could to ensure that Bay Point remains a wonderful place to live and raise a family."

He paused and looked at the audience, most of whom seemed to be listening intently. It was as though he were perched on the edge of a deep pool, everyone wondering what he would do next. Would he dive in and enter the water clean? Or would he belly flop himself right out of town?

The consequences were unknown, but he couldn't stop now. So he took a deep breath and dived in.

"This evening, I renew that promise to you. I ask you for your support during this exciting and necessary time for Bay Point. And now I'll address your questions and concerns."

Chair legs scraped against the worn linoleum floor as residents got up and formed a haphazard line behind the microphone.

Lucy spoke first. "What's going to happen to local businesses like mine?"

Gregory's stomach started to churn. He was about to go off script, sooner than he'd expected, but he'd known it would happen at some point during the meeting. It was time to tell the people of Bay Point and Vanessa the truth.

"City council and I are currently reviewing an offer from George Stodwell. If we decide to purchase his commercial buildings, they will be repaired or renovated instead of being torn down. We will be making our decision in the next few weeks."

There was a low murmur in the crowd. George Stodwell was not well liked, and some people had looks of disgust on their faces.

Gregory glanced back at Vanessa, keeping his face expressionless, even though he was worried inside. Like the others in the room, she was hearing the news about the possible sale of the buildings that housed her apartment and her store for the very first time.

Though it was dangerous to his heart to care about what she thought of him, he did care. But all she did was make a circle with her finger and mouth, "Move on."

When Gregory turned back to the crowd, the next person was already at the microphone.

"How will you preserve the historical significance of Bay Point?"

He moved from behind the podium. "Our architect has done extensive research into Bay Point's history. We don't expect there to be major changes to the existing structures, just enhancements and restoration."

A man, whom Gregory knew was a professor at the local college, was up next. "Can you talk about the lifestyle center and new housing?"

Both were a sore point with Vanessa. How many times had she said the new buildings would detract from Bay Point's charm?

"The abandoned warehouse at the corner of Magnolia and Vine Street will be torn down, and a mixed-use development will be built that will include retail, parks and playgrounds, and condominiums."

Gregory felt Vanessa's eyes on his back, accusing him, so he walked to the other end of the stage.

A woman cradling an infant approached the microphone. "I'm a single mother on a fixed income. How can I afford one of the new condos?"

Gregory smiled confidently. "We're offering a tax abatement to encourage home ownership. Affordable rentals will also be available. My vision is that Bay Point will again become what most of us already know it is—the best-kept secret on the California coast."

Maisie Barnell was next. "Young man, I just wanted to tell you that I think you are doing an outstanding job at running our town."

Jacob Billingsly strode into the room. "Yeah, running it into the ground."

Low gasps were heard in the crowd, and people turned around in their seats. Though his thunderous voice did not need a microphone, Jacob snatched it off the stand anyway, to Maisie's shocked surprise.

Gregory stole a quick glance at Vanessa, long enough to see her shrug her shoulders imperceptibly. He might not know her favorite food, but he knew what she did when she was disappointed.

They'd discussed what they would do if Billingsly showed up, but neither of them had actually believed he would. The man was so unpredictable that it was hard to know what he would do. However, they both agreed that it was extremely important that he maintain his poise and professional demeanor.

Gregory walked back to the podium, because he knew if he didn't put his hands on something in about ten seconds, they'd be around his rival's neck.

"I know what you are all thinking," Billingsly began. "But I'm not here as a candidate. I'm here as a citizen of Bay Point, and I've got a question of my own."

"A question?" Gregory asked, keeping his voice light. "The way you're holding that microphone, Billingsly, for all we know, you're going to launch into an Elvis impersonation."

Gregory knew it was an unfair jab but a well-placed one, as a few people in the crowd burst out laughing.

Jacob looked as if he spent more time in the tanning salon than on the campaign trail. His hair, though neat, was swept to the side and gelled back. He was tall and thin waisted, the type who would paunch just about the time he'd get the urge to chase younger women.

Billingsly clucked his tongue. Amplified over the microphone, it sounded like corks popping.

"Now, Mayor, don't you go crying the blues just because you're beginning to lose favor with the people. Everyone in town knows that you're about to rake them over the coals with a very bad deal."

Gregory alternated tightening and loosening his hands on the podium as he flipped through the talking points in his head.

"Over the next five years, the redevelopment plan is projected to bring over twenty-five million in additional revenue and create scores of jobs." He smiled graciously. "Now, tell me, what part of all that is a bad deal?"

Jacob ignored the question and shot back, "Why

did you wait until now to inform small-business owners that the properties they are leasing from George
Stodwell are for sale?"

Gregory locked eyes with his opponent. "The public has been informed at the proper time and will
continue to be informed on a timely basis."

"I guess that time is never," Billingsly said with a
smirk, which elicited a few nods in the crowd.

Mrs. Barnell grabbed the microphone back. "Now
you wait just a second. You have some nerve. I won't
have you disrespecting our mayor like you disrespect
your poor mother."

A look of guilt crossed Jacob's face, then quickly
disappeared. Gregory wondered how and where the
woman got her facts, but everyone in Bay Point knew
not to ask. Maisie just *knew*.

Billingsly put his hand on his chest. "I meant no
disrespect, ma'am. But with all due respect, neither
you nor the buildings you own will be affected by
the redevelopment plan. Isn't that correct?"

"Well, no," Maisie sputtered.

"So you really don't have a stake in this, do you?"

"I've lived in Bay Point for over fifty years."
Maisie gripped the microphone more tightly. "It
doesn't matter if a person owns a business or not. We
will all be affected in one way or another. I happen
to believe that the change will do us all some good."

People started talking and murmuring among
themselves. Gregory held up his hands to stop them
from grumbling.

"I want to address these accusations from my opponent. The reason I didn't inform anybody was that I only received Stodwell's offer recently. City council and I need to properly evaluate it before we make any decisions, but our initial thoughts are leaning toward purchasing the properties."

A man shouted from a row of chairs in the back, "Why is he selling, Mayor?"

He frowned. "Several tenants have not been able to make their lease payments. So rather than pursue litigation, he has decided to sell the buildings to the city."

Gregory hated airing dirty laundry, but it was necessary. The rumor mills would be spinning tonight with folks wondering who couldn't pay their rent.

"Good riddance," the same man said. "Stodwell never fixes anything anyway."

"And you think this city's administration is going to do any better?" Billingsly scoffed.

Vanessa approached the edge of the stage. "Mayor Langston isn't the enemy here."

Billingsly crossed his arms and snorted. "You're a fine one to talk, Ms. Hamilton. You must have known about this. Why didn't you tell any of your friends?"

The room went silent. All eyes were on Vanessa and Gregory.

"Actually, I didn't know. I'm assisting Mayor Langston with his reelection campaign. That's it. Though I am not an official part of his administration, I firmly believe that he cares deeply about Bay Point and its people and our future."

At Vanessa's words, Gregory felt his spirits lift. "Thank you, Ms. Hamilton. We must all stick together and not be distracted by negativity or by my opponent's desperate attempt to win votes."

Several people in the room turned and glared at Billingsly.

Gregory cleared his throat. "Our time for this evening is almost up, but we'll be having more town hall meetings in the future. We've got refreshments available across the hall. Enjoy, and thanks for being here."

At the news of free food, the crowd quickly dispersed.

Jacob Billingsly made his way to the stage, shaking hands, a robotic smile plastered on his face. Gregory and Vanessa walked down the small steps in front to meet him.

"If you wanted to have a debate, you could have asked me," Gregory said, barely able to contain his dislike of the man.

Billingsly folded his arms and grinned. "Nah. I like surprises."

"You mean attacks," Vanessa chimed in. "Too bad it didn't work."

"I made my point."

"Which is?" Gregory asked.

"You're every bit wrong for this town, Gregory. It's time for new leadership."

"And you think you're perfect for the job?" he blasted back, wishing he could wipe the smug look off Jacob's face.

"That's right. You held back critical information from this community. And when I called you out on it, you fumbled for the answer until your beautiful sidekick rescued you. Maybe she should be running for mayor."

Gregory fought the urge to clench his fists.

Mrs. Barnell spoke up. He hadn't even noticed the woman approach them. "And maybe you should learn some manners, young man."

She stuck her finger close to Jacob's face and wagged it. "If you even want a shot at running this town, running down our current leader is not the way to go about it. Maybe you do that where you came from, but here in Bay Point, we respect each other."

"And our mothers. Right?" Billingsly bowed. "I think I'll go get some of those refreshments."

Without saying another word, he turned and walked out of the room.

Gregory gritted his teeth. "Let's hope he falls into the punch bowl."

"Shush," Vanessa said. "Mrs. Barnell, you didn't hear that."

Maisie pressed her hand lightly against her ear. "Didn't hear a word, but I meant what I said, Mayor. Keep up the good work."

"Thanks for your support, Mrs. Barnell."

"It's late, Maisie," Vanessa said. "Do you want me to walk you home?"

She shook her head. "Prentice is going to take me."

They both bid her goodbye. Before they left the auditorium, Gregory turned to Vanessa. "Now do you see why I haven't held any of these meetings before?"

"You handled things well."

He shook his head, not wanting to believe her, as he began a quick mental scrutiny of the words exchanged with his rival.

"Do you think Jacob hurt my campaign even more?"

Vanessa knit her brows together. "I'm not sure. Let's split up and work the room to gauge the response."

He nodded in agreement, but just before she walked away, he grabbed her elbow.

"I just wanted to thank you for sticking with me back there. Things really could have gotten out of hand."

"Why wouldn't I? I gave you my word. And you gave me yours."

Something flickered in her eyes, challenging him to look deeper. He wanted to see, and yet he was afraid that if did, he might not ever want to leave.

Chapter 8

Thirty minutes later, Gregory and Vanessa walked out of city hall and past his car. Most people had driven to the meeting and had already gone home. The streets were deserted, and the shops were closed.

He and Vanessa were alone again, and that was just fine with him.

The dark gray concrete sidewalks appeared slick and black. Mists of fog huddled around the old-fashioned streetlamps that curled over Ocean and Magnolia Avenues, lending an eerie glow.

"It's like a ghost town around here at night," Gregory commented.

Vanessa stuck her hand out, checking for more rain, but there was nary a drop.

"You get used to it," she said with a shrug.

Her independence was appealing, even sexy. Yet ever since he'd started working with her, he'd felt a strong need to protect her. From what, he didn't know. Bay Point was incredibly safe. Petty vandalism, traffic violations and old-timers getting hit with identity theft were the only occasional crimes.

He sensed she'd been hurt, in some way, by someone.

They strolled past the carousel. Shadows clustered in the love seats and between the tarnished copper poles. Even the jewels on the horses seemed dull in the darkness.

Gregory hoped that Vanessa wouldn't launch into her "save the carousel" spiel. The hulking structure was a minefield between them that Gregory did not want to touch right now, or ever if he could help it.

He'd promised he wouldn't tear it down if she could find a way to make it work. So far she hadn't, and he wasn't going to bring it up and remind her.

"I'll walk you home," he announced suddenly, breaking the silence. "I still want to get your impressions of the meeting."

Vanessa stopped and stared at him a moment. "But your car is right here," she said, pointing to where it was parked in front of the building.

"I'd rather walk." He cocked his fedora low on his head. "These puddles make me feel like tap-dancing. All I need is a black umbrella."

"And a soundtrack," she added with a laugh. It

was low and gentle, like an invisible breeze tickling a wind chime.

Gregory wanted to offer her the crook of his arm and twirl her around, slow and easy into the night.

"Your laugh is music enough to dance to. I don't need anything else."

Except you.

She eyed him cautiously, and rightly so. He was lying to her again, and to himself. He knew he wanted more than just to hear her laugh, much more than he was willing to express.

"Are you sure you don't need anything else? What about votes?"

Gregory started to reply, then hesitated. It was difficult to tell from the tone of her voice whether she was teasing him or accusing him.

"I don't know," he finally admitted. "You tell me."

She adjusted her purse and started walking. He allowed himself a moment to watch the gentle sway of her behind and then followed, easily catching up to her.

"Billingsly's little show tonight didn't help," she said.

Gregory figured that, but deep down, what really mattered was Vanessa's confidence in him.

"What's your read on things?"

"Talking to the people at the reception, I think the harm is negligible. Most folks think he is a bully. But we really won't know for sure how they feel until election day."

"I was afraid you would say that." Gregory stuck one hand in his pocket and brought out his cell phone. "Should I call him and admit defeat?"

She stopped and peered up at him, her eyes clear and bright under the glow of the streetlamp.

"If you do that, Mayor Langston, I will quit this campaign this instant."

Relief flooded through Gregory as he put his phone away, but he also knew they were still on shaky ground. His affection for her was growing beyond that of a business relationship. He didn't want to lose her now.

"Frankly, I'm surprised to hear you say that, given what you learned tonight."

Her brows knit together, and he quelled the desire to smooth them with his thumb. "Why didn't you tell me that Stodwell offered up his buildings for sale, including mine?"

"My hands were tied."

He shrugged, hoping he didn't appear dismissive. But by the annoyed look on her face, he knew he did.

She crossed her arms, jutting her chin. "Were they? What happened to transparency, Mayor? I know I'm not part of your administration, but I need to stay informed. It makes me wonder what else you may be hiding from me."

Vanessa turned and walked away into the shadows.

He shuddered inwardly. Thank goodness her name wasn't on the list of business owners who owed taxes to the city. He'd discovered that Vanessa's father had been paying it for years.

What else was he hiding? His feelings about her were the only thing. Should he tell her that on the rare occasion when he fell immediately asleep, he awoke feeling guilty and with a raging hard-on from his dreams of her? Sharing something like that seemed silly and downright dangerous, especially since he didn't know how she felt about him.

Transparency could lead into all kinds of things he wasn't sure he could handle. Keeping his feelings secret could keep him out of trouble. At least for now.

Gregory jogged up next to her and touched her elbow to make her stop. The jolt of electricity he felt when she looked up stopped him in his tracks.

"Nothing else, Vanessa," he reassured her softly.

She nodded and stepped around a puddle, breaking contact. His legs were long, so he simply stepped over it and eagerly met up with her again.

"Except," he added, "I never told you that I like sugary cereals that make my teeth hurt, and I loathe reality television, which makes my brain hurt to even think about."

Vanessa laughed. "We all have our foibles, I guess."

"What about you?" he asked.

She kept her eyes focused ahead, and her discomfiture at his question was palpable.

"I avoid anything that ultimately results in pain."

Upon hearing her words, Gregory faltered in his

steps, almost tripping over his own feet. It was such a simple statement but loaded with complexity and darkness. He wanted to ask her what she meant by it, but he didn't dare.

He recovered quickly and they walked along together in silence, dodging puddles here and there.

They passed by a shuttered cinema where he'd mangled his first kiss, a hardware store that he'd never stepped foot into—the only hammer he liked was named MC—a day-care center housed in what used to be the town's only grocery store and an antiques shop.

Finally, they arrived at Blooms in Paradise. Gregory saw her white delivery van parked in the alley next door.

"Thank you for walking me home, Mayor. I can take it from here."

He knew she could take care of herself. She didn't need a bodyguard or a babysitter. But the truth was, he didn't want the night to end.

Gregory smiled. "I know you spend a lot of time in your store, but I also know you don't live here. I'll accompany you the rest of the way, if you don't mind," he bluffed.

She hesitated a moment, then gave him a slow nod and seemed pleased by his gesture.

They squeezed past the van and walked a short distance through the alley. The next building over, on the other side of the alley, was brick with no windows. A motion-detector light perched above the delivery entrance to the shop clicked on as they passed by, but it was not very bright.

A few feet later, Vanessa grabbed hold of the railing and climbed the steep wooden stairs leading to her apartment.

Gregory followed close behind, wondering if she would invite him in, hoping that she would.

There was a wreath of flowers on her front door, although he couldn't tell what colors they were in the dark. The single lamp in the kitchen window, framed by a ruffled curtain, cast a square of light on the wooden floor.

He couldn't see the rest of her apartment, but the kitchen looked homey.

He leaned against the railing as she fumbled in her bag for her keys. When she found them, she cried out, grabbed his hand and jerked him forward. For a small woman, she was surprisingly strong.

"Don't lean against there," she told him, her voice breathless with fear. "It's loose. I've been asking Stodwell to fix it for months, but of course, he hasn't."

He held on to her hand and jiggled the wet wood with his free one. It moved, but not enough to frighten him. Who knew what would have happened, though, if he'd put his full weight against it.

Touched by her concern, he pulled her as close to his body as he dared, leaving only a little space between them.

"Rescuing me again?"

Vanessa trembled in his arms, rippling his torso into instant awareness, but she didn't pull away. Instead she looked up at him, and he wished she would let her neatly pinned-up hair fall around her shoulders.

"What do you mean by 'again'?" she asked.

Her eyes questioned his own, beseeching him, and he wanted to make sure his answers didn't cause her to shirk away from him.

"Earlier tonight you deflected that jerk when I was so mad that I couldn't even find the words to respond. And now you've saved me from certain injury, maybe even death."

Vanessa drew in a shocked breath. "I don't want to be responsible for your demise, Mayor. I've got enough problems."

She stepped back, but not out of his embrace. "Besides, can you imagine the headlines?"

"I'd rather not," he replied grimly.

Gregory unclasped his hand from hers. It didn't make sense for him to hold it now, just as it didn't make sense to keep her in his arms.

He lowered his head slightly and sniffed, trying to be discreet and capture the smell of her hair, but he couldn't have done so without burying his nose in it.

"Thanks for saving me," he added. The words were thick and coated with gratitude. Ever since she'd stepped into his office and said yes, things had changed.

He realized how much he needed something

more than the rush that came from leading a city. He needed the rush of a woman's body laid up on his own, all night long.

But not just any woman.

Vanessa was the one he wanted.

"No problem, Mayor. But it's late, and I need to get inside."

There was a hint of resignation in her voice, and that was all he needed to hear. She broke away from him and palmed her keys in one hand. When she started to turn away, he almost let her—until something broke in him.

Gregory wrapped his arms around Vanessa's waist and pulled her to him again, but this time he wasn't going to let her go.

He eased her up against the door, out of that warm square of light, away from the view of prying eyes—though he knew that nobody was there—and into a space he created for just the two of them.

Molding her to his body slowly, amid the shadows, he instantly hardened again. It was a most immediate and pleasurable disruption, forcing him to bite back a groan.

"Before you leave, I have one question," he said, tilting her chin back. "If I kiss you, will you stop calling me Mayor?"

Without waiting for her answer, Gregory bent his head. He brushed his flesh lightly against hers, allowing himself to feel the soft velvety texture. Something rumbled between them, unseen and unbidden, yet it had the power to destroy them.

Her lips parted slightly, and he touched them with the tip of his tongue. He was holding back again, but he wanted her to be sure. She tasted sweet, like a burst of ripe melon.

Vanessa uttered a low moan. It vibrated against his lips.

"Gregory," she said against his lips. He felt her body lean against his, yielding to him, surprising him with her desire. "We can't. Someone will see."

One hand let go of her waist, and he took off his hat. With a gentle swoop, he shielded their faces, effectively cutting them off from the world.

"No one can see now."

Holding his hat in his left hand, he leaned against her, taking care not to crush her with the weight of his body.

She tilted her head and accepted his lips hungrily.

Kiss upon kiss, each one wildly rolling into the next, promiscuous and hot.

The bowl of his hat a black moon, partly covering their faces and capturing their heat in its depths. The rim, lightly pressed against their skin, a horizon, like the boundary they'd just crossed.

Her purse jutted against his abdomen, and he gently shoved it back and pulled her close with his other hand. He wanted her to feel his strength, the tension she unknowingly elicited from him.

Gregory moved his hand to the back of her waist, pulled her shirt up and away from her skirt and traveled quickly around and up to her breasts. Though she moaned when he reached them, he was disappointed to find that the round flesh was cloistered behind a padded bra.

So he sought solace in the curve of her neck and drank in the scent of her lightly perfumed skin, and he pressed his thumb against her molded bra, wishing desperately that it was her skin instead.

Her breath came out in gasps. Gasps for release? For more? He didn't know, but with every short staccato burst of air, he felt himself falling deeper into a communion of desire that ended only when her bra suddenly snapped.

Vanessa pushed him away, and he stepped back abruptly. Her eyes were blazing, and he thought she would slap him.

But she didn't. She merely tucked in her shirt and shouldered her purse.

His spirit sank into his shoes. It was as if a feather had floated before your face, and just before you grabbed hold of it, it got whisked away in the wind, and you were left to wonder. Was it even there in the first place?

The only reminder of the kiss was their breathing, and the hat he still held in his hand.

"Don't ever do that again, Gregory, or I really will quit the campaign."

His hand fell to his side, and his heart crushed

within him, surprisingly hard, as if he'd fallen over the rickety railing to the pavement below.

At least she hadn't called him Mayor.

"You want transparency, Vanessa? I'm not sorry I just kissed you now. And I don't think you are, either."

Gregory slid the hat back onto his head, adjusted the rim and eased down the stairs and into the long dark night.

Chapter 9

"Mo-om!" Vanessa half shouted.

She ran her hand lightly over the pickets of the low fence that surrounded her childhood home. It was edged with creamy-white pipestem clematis, yellow coast sunflower, which was really a shrub, and western redbud, the shade of which reminded her of her high school prom dress.

The wood, weathered gray, felt smooth and warm under her fingers. Although the aged fence sagged in some areas, the sturdiness that she loved as a child and hated as a teenager was still present. A vigilant protector, always ready to welcome her back, no matter how long she'd been away.

She unhitched the latch and bumped against the

wood with her hip until the little gate creaked and swung open.

"Mo-om, are you back there?" she called out again. As she rounded the house to the garden, the scent of roses and wildflowers drifted through the midmorning haze into her nose.

"Hush, girl," her mother scolded, rising to her knees. "You know I am."

Jewel Hamilton dropped a little weeding tool into a plastic bucket, then lifted one gloved hand and raised the flap on her wide-brimmed hat.

The crow's-feet around her eyes lifted in the muted sunlight. Her mother had no fear of getting old, referring to her few wrinkles as God's kisses, a soothing testament to the hardships and the blessings of life.

Vanessa admired the plant she had been weeding, which was bursting with violet-blue flowers. "It reminds me of fireworks."

"It's beautiful," her mother remarked. "And a pain to maintain. Just ask my knees."

Vanessa gave her a hug. "You wouldn't have it any other way."

She smiled. "You're right." Her mother looked around the garden, like a queen surveying her kingdom. "My plants never have an opinion. I talk. They listen."

"The perfect relationship." Vanessa grinned. "But, Mom, you love to talk to anyone, not just plants."

Jewel slipped off her gloves and dropped them

into the bucket, where they landed soundlessly. "I suppose I do. But my plants are the only ones who don't argue back."

Vanessa followed her mother to the small patio. Sure, her mother talked to her plants. But even more important, she always talked, and listened, to her. So many of her friends weren't close with their mothers. Thankfully, she was.

Jewel was born in the late '50s. She was a quirky dresser and had an earthy beatnik-like appeal. She was also genuinely kind, not the stilted gesture of political correctness that passed for that type of character today.

As a kid, Vanessa was often embarrassed by her mother's outspokenness. How she attached herself to various causes, most of which people had never even heard of, many of which folks couldn't care less about. But now Jewel's activism made her proud, and a little bit envious.

Though she cared deeply about her causes, her mother had always managed to separate herself from them. On the other hand, Vanessa got emotionally attached to whatever and whomever she chose to get involved with, political or not.

Thinking briefly of Gregory and the kisses they shared the evening before—call it lust or call it longing—she had a long way to go before she could separate from her growing feelings for him.

They had an election to win.

She had a carousel to save.

Jewel checked her watch. "What are you doing here in the middle of a Saturday morning?"

Vanessa took a step back. "Can't I just come home and visit my own mother without a reason?" she asked in a hurt voice.

Jewel eyed her in that curious way that mothers do, which is designed to invoke either instant guilt or guilty tears or both.

"Sure, but I can tell by the look on your face that something's wrong. Besides, aren't you supposed to be at the shop?"

"I closed up for the morning," she replied carefully. "That's one benefit of owning my own business. I call all the shots."

Jewel, who was busy brushing the dirt from her pants, seemed unconvinced. "And you also lose all the money."

"Ugh. Don't remind me." Vanessa bit her lip, unsure if she should change the subject. "I was surprised you weren't at the town hall meeting last night. I thought you cared about the community."

"I thought the same thing about you, Vanessa," her mother replied. She sat down on a patio chair and gestured to an empty one across from her. "How could you be helping that man? He's trying to ruin our town, you know!"

Vanessa sat down and sighed. Though she hated the disappointment she'd heard in her voice, she'd expected this reaction from her mother, who had a general disdain for politics and politicians.

"There's nothing inherently wrong with Gregory."

Unless you count being drop-dead gorgeous. That was his only crime, besides keeping her awake all night with the memory of his kisses.

"Of course not," Jewel scolded. "But his redevelopment plan is a mistake. Those new buildings will be too contemporary looking."

Vanessa almost laughed out loud. Didn't she say something similar to Gregory on the day he first walked into her shop and asked her to be his campaign manager? It seemed like a lifetime ago that she'd blasted away at his plans.

Now all she could remember was his muscular body pressed against hers and that hat perched upon his head when he left her.

"You mean ugly?"

Jewel nodded as she got up. "Exactly."

"If it makes you feel any better, Gregory shared the preliminary designs with me, and it appears that the architect is at least trying to respect the historical integrity of downtown Bay Point."

Her mother turned on the spigot attached to the house and started washing her hands.

"That's all well and good, until the contractors roll in with their chemical-laden building materials." Jewel turned to look back at her daughter. "Do you know what's in drywall these days?"

Vanessa fought from rolling her eyes. Sometimes her mother's zeal for the earth seemed like downright paranoia.

If it had been anyone else, Vanessa would have accused her of listening to Jacob Billingsly's outrageous claims that the redevelopment plan would be an environmental disaster.

But her mother had likely done some research on her own.

"If you care so much, then why weren't you at the meeting?"

Jewel walked toward her and wiped her hands on a clean towel. "Because I think what you're doing is wrong."

There was a pitcher of iced tea on the patio table. Vanessa poured two glasses, handed one to her mother and gave her an incredulous look.

"It's wrong to fight for what I believe in?" she stated, trying not to sound sarcastic. "That's a pretty comical statement coming from an activist. Would you rather I work for Billingsly?"

Jewel made a face. "That man? He's worse. I don't care for his tactics, and his claims have no basis in fact." She sipped her tea thoughtfully. "He's also a bigger threat to Bay Point than Gregory is."

Vanessa was drinking her beverage and almost choked at her mother's words. "No way. He has no power, and he'll never get elected. Gregory will win."

If he didn't, she knew she would never forgive herself.

"How can you be so sure?" Jewel asked, narrowing her eyes.

"Because I believe in—" And she stopped herself.

She wanted to say that she believed in him. It was the truth, but somehow saying those words to her mother made it more real. More permanent.

"Because I believe in the power of the people," she finished. "They'll choose the best man for the job. Most know it's not Jacob Billingsly, especially after what he pulled last night."

Jewel twisted her mouth to the side. "I heard Maisie Barnell got in his face. He made a lot of enemies last night."

"And perhaps a few friends," Vanessa added. "There's always a few haters in the house, but it doesn't matter. Mayor Langston will prevail."

Her last statement was delivered with a vehemence that surprised even herself. A little bit of that "he's my man and he's the best" attitude had slowly crept into her system, settled into her belly and put a fire into her heart.

And if Vanessa mistakenly thought her mother didn't notice the change in her, it was because she was too caught up in the moment, too busy trying to hold on to the memory of last night to care.

Jewel set her empty glass on the table. "I just don't want you to get hurt. Remember what happened before? When you moved back home from LA, you were—"

"A wreck. I remember, Mom."

She bit the inside of her lip. The rejection she'd felt at the hands of her former boss-turned-lover was, at that time, mightier than anything else that she'd faced. Coming home had been only the beginning of the battle.

"I don't want you to go through that again."

Their eyes met, and there was a tremor in her mother's voice that made Vanessa want to break down and cry.

As much as Jewel loved the fight for a good cause, like most people, she wanted only peace and harmony at home. Conflict within her family was like an invasive plant that needed to be rooted out or, better yet, treated before it even started.

Whenever Vanessa and her brother got into an argument that lasted longer than her mother thought it should, she would pull them both into the kitchen to make homemade chicken soup. She called it "the Great Equalizer," and by the time they had finished making it and sat down to eat, Vanessa and her brother had forgotten what they'd been fighting about in the first place.

Looking back on it now, making chicken soup was also a way for her mother to try to make up for all the time their father didn't spend with them. Though he loved his wife and children, he was always at the hospital. If there was leftover soup when he came home, he knew that another conflict had been eradicated like some sort of disease, and his family, although he knew they missed him terribly, was still intact.

"I'm going to be okay, Mom. Really," she said, as much to convince herself as to convince her mother.

"Just don't get involved," Jewel warned.

Too late, Vanessa thought. Last night had changed everything.

"Why did Mayor Langston approach you, anyway?"

"His father told him to call Dad, who told him about my previous work in politics. And because it appears I'm the only one in town qualified, he offered me the job."

Thank God her father didn't know the painful little details of her time in Los Angeles.

Jewel nodded. "Even though you're his campaign manager, surely you don't believe the mayor's plan is a good thing for Bay Point. Do you?"

Vanessa paused. If city council decided to accept Stodwell's offer, her building would be owned by the city. No doubt about it—things in Bay Point were going to be different, whether she or anyone else liked it or not.

But if she showed too much allegiance with the mayor, her mother would launch into a speech about big government intruding into everyday lives, and Vanessa didn't want to argue with her now. She didn't have time to make chicken soup today. She had deliveries to make, and the kiss of a lifetime to remember.

"Even though I've seen the blueprints, I do agree with you about the lifestyle center," she finally admitted. "I really don't like contemporary architecture."

Her mother clapped her hands and smiled. "At

least we agree about something. But I still don't understand why you're doing this."

"To save the carousel. He wants to tear it down, Mama."

Even saying the words *tear it down* tore Vanessa's heart into shreds.

Her mother gave her an odd look. "But the carousel is only one aspect of downtown. There are so many more structures that will be affected."

Vanessa pressed on, keeping her emotions in check. "I know, but I feel that it's the most important part. I know it sounds silly, but I really feel that the carousel is what holds this whole town together."

"Was the demolition of it a discussion point at the town hall meeting?"

"Actually, nobody brought it up. But that's only because the redevelopment plan was more top of mind," she replied hastily.

At least, that was what Vanessa hoped. She couldn't be the only one in town who valued the longevity and the memories of the Bay Point Carousel.

Vanessa leaned her head against the chair and tilted her chin to the sky. "Remember all the good times we had there?"

Jewel smiled. "Your father would always take you two for a ride when he was home."

"And then we'd head over to Ruby's afterward." Vanessa shut her eyes and sighed. "I never could decide which one was better—seeing Daddy or having double-dip strawberry ice cream. I guess both were a treat."

Jewel laughed and closed her eyes, felt the sun on her cheeks as her mind traveled back to the years of raising two kids with a loving husband who, due to his work, was rarely home.

The simmering anger during the day, followed by the crippling guilt at night when he still wasn't there. She knew where he was and what he was doing. It wasn't as if he were with another woman or drinking or gambling or running around town. He was saving lives.

Still, it was a vicious emotional cycle, broken only by endless joy when he finally walked through the door.

The carousel was the one place where she could guarantee that her husband would be present for his children. There was no empty place at the table, no bedtime story not read, no homework not done, no missed baseball games or ballet recitals. The carousel was the one place where they could be a family.

She opened her eyes again. "Those were good times. I understand why you'd want to keep the carousel intact. But don't get so caught up that you begin to lose sight of why you were fighting in the first place."

Vanessa sat up straight in her chair. "I'll be okay, Mom."

"What have I always taught you? Never trust a politician."

"But Gregory isn't just a politician. He grew up in Bay Point."

"But is he rooted in the right things?" Jewel asked. "That's what you've got to find out."

Her mother, thankfully, changed the subject to something they both loved and could agree on: gardening.

As they were talking, Vanessa admired the backyard. Some of the trees and perennials planted by her great-grandfather, who was the original owner of the house, were still thriving. Fifty years from now, even ten years from now, would the same be said of Bay Point?

A short time later, Vanessa hugged her mother goodbye and walked around the house to her car. She got in and was about to put the key into the ignition when she stopped suddenly.

What was it that her mother had said? Something about not losing sight of why she was fighting for something?

She lay her forehead on the steering wheel and two fingers on her lips, trying to remember Gregory's kiss. Last night it felt as if it was meant to be.

But right now it was unbelievable that it would be anything but the tender wisp of a moment. Like hearing the ocean in a seashell.

Vanessa remembered the kiss and wanted to revel in it, but the memory was fading quickly. She wished she could put a picket fence around it. Protect it from the elements of doubt and distrust, promises made

and broken. And she knew there could never be another moment like it without risk.

The issue wasn't the carousel. It was whether or
not she was willing to take another chance with her
heart.

Chapter 10

Gregory leaned against the street pole on Ocean Avenue across from Blooms in Paradise. With his hands in his pockets, he admired the tall blue tin vases lined up in a row outside the window like little guardsmen.

There were a few customers milling about, selecting from an array of ready-made bundles of colorful flowers, and then disappearing inside. He waited until they had all left and then he hurried across the street.

A bell announced him with a cheerful jingle as he shut the door behind him. Vanessa was nowhere in sight. He was flipping the sign from Open to Closed when he heard her voice.

"What do you think you're doing?"

He cringed inwardly at the sharpness in her tone. It was as if he'd stepped onto sacred ground without her permission.

Gregory smiled at her, but it was not returned, and it felt as if his heart had been sucker punched.

"You're officially on break," he said, hoping his pleasant tone would ease the tension between them.

Vanessa had spoken to him from the doorway that was in the back of the store, just behind the main counter, which appeared to lead to another room.

Now she whisked around the counter, and Gregory felt the air swoosh as she quickly walked past him and flipped the sign back to Open.

"I own my own business. I can't afford to take breaks."

"And I'm not leaving until I get some answers," he replied in a calm voice, flipping the sign back to Closed. "The only way I can do that is if I can grab some uninterrupted time with you."

Both of their hands were raised, their fingers poised over the sign, their opposition framed by the shop window. If someone had painted them, the work might have been called *Still Life of a Power Struggle.* Their standoff felt awkward and unseemly and completely opposite from what Gregory wanted.

He didn't want to fight with her; he wanted to care for her. He dropped his hand to the side first, and she followed suit.

Vanessa's eyes darted to the sign, and Gregory felt a twinge of guilt. He knew it wasn't right to deprive her of potential customers, but it wasn't as if he'd locked the door.

"Don't worry," he assured her. "This won't take long."

"You said you wanted answers." Her upper lip quivered. "Answers to what?"

Gregory absently reached up to take off his hat but forgot that he hadn't worn it today. Not wanting to appear foolish, he ran his hand over his head instead.

"Why you've been avoiding me ever since Friday night."

Her eyes searched the floor briefly, and then she raised her chin. "I've answered your emails. I do have other responsibilities."

"Remember that little surprise Billingsly pulled at the first town hall meeting? We need a plan of attack so that he doesn't do that again at the next one."

Gregory was relieved when she nodded in agreement.

"Did you get any more feedback from members of the community?"

He told her about the many requests to see the blueprints of the lifestyle center and condos.

"A scale model would be even more useful," she said, moving away from the door. "It will make the redevelopment plan more real and bring it to life for everyone."

Vanessa was dressed in skinny black jeans and a faded T-shirt of an '80s band that was popular when they were both still babes in a crib.

The shirt hugged her curves as if it wouldn't let go and stopped abruptly at her waist. The jeans were tight, but she moved so easily in them.

Gregory couldn't recall ever seeing her in such a casual outfit that was not her flower shop uniform. He loved the look and found it difficult not to stare.

"That's a terrific idea, Vanessa. I can put you in touch with the architect, and you can arrange it."

She opened one of the refrigerated cases, and the rush of cold air matched the chill in the room. When she was finished neatening some of the flowers, she turned around but would not look at him. She held a small cluster of pink roses, the same pale pink as the color of her lipstick. She was frowning.

"What's wrong?" he asked.

"They're starting to wilt."

She walked over, and he was momentarily distracted by the easy sway of her hips. He was taken aback when she thrust the flowers close to his face.

"See?"

Gregory detected just a tiny bit of curl in the petals. Otherwise the roses looked perfect to him, just like the woman standing in front of him.

His eyes drifted from the flowers to her full lips, like a searchlight sweeping across a dark harbor, ready to discover and to explore.

"They look beautiful."

He meant the woman, not the flowers, but her mouth pursed tightly, as if he were talking about something else entirely.

"I can't help you, Mayor."

He heard her words. Little bullets of destruction.

And it saddened him that she'd reverted back to formality. How he ached for her to moan his given name.

His eyes snapped up to hers, which were clear and determined.

"What are you saying, Vanessa? Did you forget that we have an election to win?"

The roses brushed against the side of her jeans, releasing a soft fragrance into the air. The barely wilted petals remained intact on their stems.

"We?" Vanessa repeated. "You have to win the election. I have to run my flower shop."

Her tone sounded as isolating as their careers, and seconds later it reverberated into his heart as fear. He'd been afraid that this would happen. Kissing her had been impulsive and pleasurable and a risk he'd gladly take again.

Gregory crossed his arms over his chest. "So you have a business to run, or are you just running away from me?"

They stood only a foot apart, yet a deep chasm existed between them, made worse when Vanessa wouldn't meet his eyes.

Her grip on the roses relaxed a little, and he reached out and touched her hair. "I've missed our morning meetings, Vanessa."

She lifted her chin, eyeing him warily. "I think you're just making up excuses."

"I don't need an excuse. I just miss you."

"Stop talking like that!"

Vanessa stepped back. Her eyes flashed a warning, and Gregory knew that winning her love wouldn't be easy. He was the kind of guy who kept his feelings private. Even before he became a politician, he'd found it hard to open up to people, especially women.

He wanted to open up to her, but he couldn't until she realized that his heart wasn't a platform to be mocked and mangled.

"Like what? I'm telling you the truth."

He didn't know which hurt more. Getting up the courage to tell her that he missed her or hearing his words thrown back in his face. Though he knew she wasn't trying to hurt him intentionally, her words still stung.

She walked around the counter and slapped the bouquet down roughly. Petals scattered across the glass, their fragrance escaping into the brittle air between them.

"It's not right. I can't be involved with you right now, like this, not after the other night."

He put his palms flat on the counter and leaned in close. Her upper lip trembled as she met his eyes.

"So you've decided to walk away. Because I kissed you. Is that it?"

Vanessa mimicked his stance, arms locked straight, and leaned in. "No. I'm walking away because it's the right thing to do. For both of us."

He watched her mouth tremble and then shook his head. "That doesn't make any sense, Vanessa. There's no ring on your finger. There's no man knocking at your door, except me."

She pushed herself away from the counter. "As I recall, you didn't knock. You barged right in."

"Would you have let me in any other way?"

They both knew the answer.

Her brow furrowed. "It doesn't matter now."

She began to pick up the petals, one by one. Her fingers skittered across the counter as though they were on fire.

"Look, Vanessa, like I told you that night, I'm not sorry I kissed you. I'm still not. I had hoped you wouldn't be, either."

His hand caught hers, clenched with a fistful of petals, and she exhaled in surprise.

Again he waited for her to admonish him or to tell him that she wasn't sorry about their kiss. Anything was better than silence.

"What about the carousel?" she finally asked.

The carousel? He clenched his jaw. *Doesn't she care about me?*

He released her hand, took a moment to answer, to tuck his emotions away once again.

"It's still slated to be demolished as planned."

Vanessa opened her fist and dumped a wad of crushed petals on the glass, then disappeared through the doorway.

He raised his voice slightly, wanting to be heard but still not sure whether he should follow her.

"But if you quit now, there's no chance it will be saved."

"Why's that?" she called out.

Gregory decided that she didn't sound as though she were in a basement. So he got up and followed her.

Just as he was about to go through the door, Vanessa reappeared and they almost collided.

"Why's that?" she repeated, her voice a little weaker.

Gregory grabbed her elbow to steady her. This time she didn't wrench away from his touch. "Because the reason for the promise that I made in the first place will be gone. That reason is you." He released her and peered over her head.

"So, this is where the magic happens, huh?"

Vanessa stepped aside, allowing him to enter the room. "No, this is where the hard work happens."

Similarly to the front of the store, there were two additional double-door refrigerated cases filled with a variety of flowers.

But in the back, on one side there were also giant rolls of wrapping paper, sheets of tissue paper and spools of ribbons, all in many colors and patterns. A helium tank was in the corner, but Gregory didn't see any balloons for sale in the main store area.

Along the other wall there was a farmhouse-style

sink and a butcher-block counter. Gregory ran his hand over the smooth wood.

"That's where I do most of my floral arranging," she murmured.

"This space is like an artist's canvas," he remarked. "Where you can, and do, create beautiful pieces."

Vanessa shrugged her shoulders, and she seemed embarrassed.

Gregory was glad that she didn't deny her creative talents. He rubbed his arms. The room was chilly, not unlike Vanessa's mood earlier, but she was beginning to thaw. Now was the time to get her back into his corner.

"Vanessa, I really need your help and support on this campaign."

He didn't want to lose her, not as a campaign manager, nor as a friend. Not now. Maybe not ever.

"Won't you please reconsider?"

When she didn't answer, Gregory noticed a picture on the wall above her head and walked around her for a closer look. It was a framed black-and-white photo of the Bay Point Carousel, and it appeared to be very old. He held his breath a moment in disbelief.

"Where did you get this photo?" He pointed at it. "I called all over town for one and was told that none existed."

Vanessa swiveled around and gave him an odd look. "It belonged to my grandfather, and he passed it down to me. Why did you need it?"

"The architect wanted to see a picture of the original structure."

"But why?"

Her eyes widened, and he could see hope within them. He hesitated to tell her more. But he was afraid he already had.

"There was a point where he thought that if the carousel could be torn down and moved, it could be included in the blueprints for the new municipal complex."

"And," she said, urging him on, "what happened?"

"He did some research and discovered that it would be cheaper just to tear it down."

She shook her head. "You made the right decision."

He blew out a slow breath. "I'm surprised to hear you say that."

"Moving the carousel would never work. It needs to stay right where it is, right where it's been for generations."

"So you haven't changed your mind about it?" he asked.

"Not at all. In fact, every day this picture makes me feel even more confident that saving the carousel is the right thing to do."

It has the opposite effect on me, Gregory thought as he peered at the photo even more closely. Though it was taken in the daylight, the effect the image had on him nearly knocked him to his knees, for in it he saw saccharine-sweet painted-on smiles. Artificial happiness. Searing disappointment.

Incredible loss.

"When you were growing up, did you ever think you'd want to remember the past?" he asked her suddenly.

"What do you mean?"

He shook his head. "Never mind. But you made a promise. If you quit the campaign, then the carousel will be demolished."

She took a step closer to him. "Why, Gregory?" Her voice was nearly pleading. "Why do you hate the carousel so much?"

"Because you haven't given me a reason to save it," he answered quietly, before leaving her workroom.

He picked up the clump of rose petals on the counter and pocketed them, and when he left, it was as if he'd had a near miss with a bad dream.

Promise or no promise, the past would not come back to haunt him, not if he could help it. No, he would be the first one to hoist the sledgehammer.

Chapter 11

Vanessa stepped out of her apartment and locked the door. She flipped the hood of her black windbreaker over her head to protect her hair from the light rain and took a cleansing breath of the fresh air.

She was on her way to Lucy's to have a community meeting about the carousel. She'd told a few people at the flower shop today about the impromptu gathering and was relying on the Bay Point rumor mill to spread the word.

As she made her way down the rickety stairs to the alley, her heart felt as miserable as the weather. The rain would probably keep people away, and besides, Gregory still planned on tearing it down.

Now on the pavement, she shoved her hands in her pockets and tilted her chin up to her apartment.

Maybe she should just go home, make herself a cup of hot cocoa with loads of delicious whipped cream and forget about the carousel—and Gregory.

Ever since the night Gregory had kissed her, she couldn't leave or come home without thinking of him.

Raindrops sprinkled across her nose. She rubbed them away and trudged on. She had no business kissing the man that night and no business being disappointed that he hadn't kissed her that afternoon. Would she ever stop being attracted to him?

Likely not, she thought as she passed her delivery van. It was something she'd have to learn to live with, much like her desire for expensive handbags, which she could never afford.

The kiss had been a mistake, but so was almost quitting the campaign today. What had she been thinking? She'd almost walked away due to fear about her growing feelings for him.

Gregory was right. She hadn't given him a good reason to save the carousel, but she hoped tonight would be a start.

Vanessa reached the sidewalk and frowned. Lucy had graciously offered to close down her restaurant so that the meeting could be held there. But no cars were parked outside, and the shades were pulled down over the windows. But how could that be? She couldn't be the only one in town who cared about the carousel, could she?

A lump bubbled up in her throat as she made her way across the street. She twisted the doorknob of the restaurant, and when she opened the door, the lights flickered on.

"Surprise!" a multitude of voices, young and old, shouted.

The lump in her throat dissipated, and her tennis shoes screeched to a halt on the worn tile floor. Raucous claps of applause pelted the air with so much energy that Vanessa couldn't help but smile.

"What is this?" she cried, her eyes welling with tears at the sight of so many people in the room. Every seat and booth was filled. The stools along the bar were all taken, and there were folks standing along the back wall.

"I wished for a crowd, and now you're all here," Vanessa said, rubbing her hands dramatically over the large crystal ball near the doorway. "This thing really does work!"

Lucy came forth and gave her a hug. She smelled of coffee and cinnamon and simple blessings.

"Thank you!" Vanessa whispered against her ear. "When I walked over and saw all the shades down, I thought the worst."

Lucy released her with a knowing smile. "Come on out of that rain, child." She gestured to the crowd. "All of your friends are here."

Vanessa shrugged out of her coat and hung it onto a rack with the others. The restaurant was a sanctuary of cozy warmth, and the scent of fresh coffee and peach pie floated through the air, making her stomach rumble.

Maisie approached and gave her a quick hug. "We're here to help you save the carousel, right, everyone?"

The crowd responded with more claps and cheers. Vanessa's heart surged with gratitude. She had never felt more love and appreciation for her town than she did right at that moment.

She walked over and stood in front of the counter that held the cash register. Faces turned toward her, anticipatory with interest. Most she recognized, but there were a few she did not.

"Thank you, everyone, for coming out in this weather this evening. I can't tell you how much I appreciate each and every one of you."

She cleared her throat. "As you know, our beloved carousel is in danger of being demolished as part of Mayor Langston's redevelopment plan and to make way for a new municipal building."

A couple of people in the room booed their disapproval, and she paused.

"Some of you have grown up with the carousel. Others may have discovered it for the first time. But the fact that we are all here shows how important it is. The carousel is part of our past, our present and, with your help, will be a part of our future."

"How do we save it?" said Henry Wexler, owner of the local antiques shop, located a few doors down from Blooms in Paradise.

"We need to clean it up. Make it sparkle," Vanessa replied.

He stroked his salt-and-pepper beard and considered her request. "Normally, I would advise people to leave antiquities alone, but in this case, I agree with you. A little sprucing up, done carefully and in keeping with the original design, couldn't hurt."

A man raised his hand in the back. "With the carousel being over a hundred years old, I'm betting we're not going to be able to match the paint with something from the hardware store."

Vanessa nodded. "You're right."

"Plus, each horse is unique and there are so many colors it would take weeks to paint all of them. How much time do we have?" Maisie asked.

"Not enough," she admitted. "We need to complete the cleanup in no more than two weekends. Plus, you're right about the paint colors."

Lucy walked over and handed Vanessa a fresh cup of coffee. "But all the horses do have one thing in common. They all have gold saddles!"

"And the poles are gold, too!" said Mariella, Gregory's assistant, from where she was perched on a bar stool, her son next to her.

A ray of hope sprang into Vanessa's heart. "If we can paint the poles and the saddles, that might be enough to snazzy up the carousel a bit."

"I can get the paint matched," Henry offered. "A friend of mine owes me a favor. I'll have to let him beat me at chess, but it will be worth it if the carousel will still be around so that my baby granddaughter can ride it when she grows up."

Vanessa clapped her hands together with excitement. "Now we're rolling. Who else has an idea?"

Clarisse James, the wife of one of the deacons at Bay Point Baptist, stood up. "It's all well and good to make the carousel look pretty again, but if it doesn't run, it will be a lot of wasted effort."

"Why would anybody want to ride that old thing anyway?" Mariella's son jeered.

Vanessa knew he was trying to find his place among the social strata of Bay Point's teenagers, and that he'd probably rather be home playing video games.

"Hush," Mariella said. "Lots of people do, including me, but since we've moved here, I've actually never seen it working," she announced to the crowd.

"You're not the only one," Clarisse said with a wry smile.

Vanessa's heart fell. She needed to find someone to actually fix the carousel and make it run—and run safely.

Gregory had said that the one person who did know how to repair it had moved away. Even if they had someone on staff, there was no money in the budget to pay them for the work.

A hush fell over the room as everyone racked their brains.

"My uncle can fix cars," a young teenage girl offered shyly. "I don't know what powers a carousel, but it has to be similar to an engine, right?"

Vanessa smiled. "Thank you. I don't know, either,

but I think we probably need a different type of repair person for this work."

Prentice spoke up from the back of the room. "I know somebody who can help."

Clarisse turned in her seat and glared at him. Everyone in town knew that she had been the most vocal in ousting Prentice from the church.

"You do?" Clarisse asked with disdain. "Who?"

Prentice shifted in his chair. "Just leave it to me," he instructed. "Tell me the date and the time, and I'll make sure this person is there."

Clarisse laughed. "And you expect us to trust you?"

Nobody said a word and Vanessa felt bad for Prentice, but she knew that he never backed down from anything. And she knew from Gregory that though he was sometimes lazy, he was as good as his word.

Prentice clicked his tongue against his teeth. "Nope, Deaconess James, I expect you to trust God."

Many in the room were having trouble holding back a laugh or a smile. What could Clarisse possibly say to that? Vanessa wondered. She could almost see the steam coming from Clarisse's ears, but she only exhaled loudly and turned around in her chair.

"Thank you for offering your assistance, Prentice. I'll get back to you with the dates as soon as I have them."

Vanessa clapped her hands again and addressed her friends and fellow citizens. "What other ideas do you have to build support for our little movement?"

"Why don't we have some sort of community day," Ruby suggested. "It'll be a way for the entire Bay Point community to come together."

People started talking among themselves with excitement.

"It can't be just about the carousel," Henry said.

"We can do free health screenings," said one woman, whom Vanessa recognized as a nurse from the hospital.

"And have concession stands and baked goods," Lucy added, "from our local restaurants and other groups."

"What about rides?" said Josh.

"We don't have any money to rent them," Vanessa said. "But maybe we can figure out a way to have games for the kids."

"Face painting is always a hit," Mariella added.

"But first you need a place to hold the event. How about the parking lot of Bay Point High?" Maisie said. "It's plenty big, and if it rains, we could use the gym."

Vanessa's head began to swim with all the possibilities. "We'll need lots of volunteers."

Lucy handed Vanessa a pen. "I've got lots of paper."

She led her to a table. "Everyone who wants to be a part of the community day and the carousel cleanup days, stop over here and give Vanessa your name and phone number. When you're done, please enjoy a complimentary cup of coffee and slice of pie."

A crowd gathered around the table, and the mood was merry and festive.

Minutes later the door to the restaurant opened and Jacob Billingsly sauntered in. Lucy, who was serving slices of pie from behind the bar, hurried up to greet him.

"The shades were drawn. I was coming to see if anything was wrong, and I walk into a party," he said in the gloating tone that Vanessa hated.

"The restaurant is closed tonight for a private event," Lucy explained patiently. "Come back in the morning for breakfast."

"No," Jacob said. "I think I'll hang around here for a while."

Vanessa got up. "You're welcome to stay if you'd like to join us. We're going to be cleaning up the carousel in a few weeks."

"That old merry-go-round?" Jacob scoffed. "It's outlived its usefulness, and it's a pain in the butt to keep running. That's one point the mayor and I agree on," he added.

"I never thought of the carousel as useful," Vanessa commented. "Regardless, all of us in this room value it, and we'll be working hard to change the mayor's mind."

Jacob's eyes scanned the room, and he didn't see people as much as he saw potential votes. "Maybe you can change mine first, Ms. Hamilton."

She handed him a pen, ignored the twinge of guilt and smiled. "The more, the merrier."

Chapter 12

Vanessa pinned the last bit of purple ribbon to the edge of the booth and nodded with satisfaction. She could have used some help decorating, but her volunteers were helping somewhere else at the festival. Somehow she'd managed to do it herself.

"The Save the Carousel Committee has really outdone themselves, haven't they?"

Gregory's voice wrapped around her like silk, heightening her senses, but she couldn't tell if he was complimenting or making fun of her. She plucked a small reel of ribbon from her mouth, which had served as her extra hand, and put it down on the table.

"Right now I'm a committee of one. Are you here to help, Mayor? Or hurl insults?"

His lips edged up to a smile, which he tossed at her carelessly. "To help, of course."

She put the reel of ribbon on the table. "Even if it's something you don't believe in?" she challenged.

But before he could answer, a sudden breeze blew one of the purple flowers from the top corner of the booth. It rustled like a flag briefly before starting to make its descent to the ground.

"I'll get it," Vanessa exclaimed breathlessly.

She extended her arm to grab the decoration before it hit the pavement, but before she knew what was happening, Gregory had reattached it to the booth's frame.

He caught her hand in his.

"Will you take that as a yes?"

She sucked in a breath. "I guess I don't have any other choice, do I?"

Gregory stared into her eyes, and it seemed as if she was caught in their depths, until a child ran by and broke the spell.

Reluctantly, he let go of her hand and she entered the tented booth. She sat down on a brown metal chair and began to straighten some pamphlets, trying to ignore the gorgeous man standing right in front of her.

Today he was dressed in light blue slacks and a crisp white polo that accentuated his masculine physique. He'd traded in his black fedora for a linen one, which made him look as though he were permanently on vacation.

His body was partially blocking the sunlight from shining on her, but he still drew a slow heat that spread from her toes to her fingertips.

Gregory's presence always resulted in subliminal longing that she tried to deny, but it was always there.

"So you can catch wayward ribbons. What else can you do?"

He crossed his arms. "I've been trying to catch you, but so far I've been an epic failure."

She tilted her chin at him and crooked her finger. "Can I give you a tip?"

He bent and leaned forward so eagerly that she had to hold back a smile.

"I don't want to be caught," she whispered.

Her words were a lie, of course, but Vanessa felt that she needed to keep some kind of boundary between them. In public, at least, but not in her heart.

Gregory straightened abruptly, cupped a hand to his chest and staggered back, as if he were wounded.

"Way to break a man's game!"

"I could bring you flowers," she offered, her voice more seductive than she intended.

He squatted before the table until his face was eye level with hers. "To force me to give up or to make me keep trying?"

"I guess you took my advice earlier this week to heart," she said, abruptly changing the subject.

"To move heaven and earth to get here?" Gregory nodded. "I didn't need an excuse or a reason. I just made it happen." Suddenly he turned his head and quickly stood again.

"The community day was a great idea, Vanessa."

His voice seemed loud and overly stilted in her ears, confusing her until she saw a group of people walking by. Even though they didn't appear to be paying attention to what was going on at the Save the Carousel booth, Vanessa was glad that the mayor wasn't taking any chances.

"Unfortunately, I can't claim responsibility for it, but everyone has really rallied together to pull it off," she replied, though not as loudly.

In addition to booths featuring health screenings, church groups and other community-based organizations, there were concession stands offering sugary delights from Ruby's pastry shop, Lucy's famous jerk chicken sandwiches and wares from other local vendors.

A group of high schoolers were running activities for the kids, including face painting, games and crafts.

The weather was beautiful and clear, with sunny skies. People had started to arrive and were visiting the booths, lining up for food or just talking with their neighbors.

It was going to be a great day, Vanessa decided, especially now that Gregory was here. He'd told her that he wasn't sure if he was going to make it, due to an existing conflict.

He lowered his voice to a tone meant only for her. "Everything looks great, including you."

"Mayor Langston!"

They both turned to see Jacob Billingsly striding toward them. "Are you now a part of the committee, too?"

Gregory eyed his opponent. "What do you mean by 'too'?"

"I officially joined the cause," Jacob announced. He gestured toward the sign on the booth. "And a great one it is, I might add."

He looped his arm around Vanessa's shoulders. She tried not to cringe. "The Bay Point Carousel is the ticket to putting our town back on the map."

"And putting you into office?" Gregory smirked.

Jacob grinned. "You know, Mayor, there's something about that carousel that brings people together, and if it brings people to the polls, then all the better."

He gave Vanessa's shoulder a tight squeeze. "Our little florist here opened my eyes to all sorts of possibilities. Too bad she didn't open yours."

Jacob winked and strolled away, greeting and shaking hands with people walking by.

Gregory swiveled around. "What the hell was that all about?"

She smiled weakly, wishing she could go home and take a shower. Jacob Billingsly was a snake of the worst kind, but he had purchased the booth for the committee. The only caveat was that he have a place to display his campaign materials.

"You'd be surprised at how many people actually love the carousel, Gregory. We already have a ton of people protesting the demolition."

She grabbed a clipboard from the table. "I've already collected a ton of signatures."

"How many?" he asked, trying to peer over her clipboard, which she quickly stowed underneath the table.

His eyes widened when she put a stack of postcards on the table urging people to "Vote for Change, Vote for Billingsly."

Gregory put his hands up, and the look on his face was one of shock and hurt, neither of which she had meant to cause.

"Whoa! Forget about the carousel for a minute, will you?"

Gregory's hand slid over hers, and the motion, while subtly possessive, also felt oddly comforting.

"What are you doing with Billingsly?" he demanded. "Are you working for him now?"

From his mildly jealous tone, she suspected that he wasn't concerned only about the ramifications to his campaign of what he thought was a new allegiance to his rival.

Could he actually care about her?

The notion made her skin tingle, but she quickly slipped her hand away when a group of volunteers approached the booth. As Gregory greeted them, she handed each person a clipboard and a pen, with instructions to gather as many signatures as possible.

When they were alone again, Vanessa stood up and walked around to the front of the booth. She wanted to ensure that they would not be caught in an awkward situation.

"I'm not working for Jacob's campaign. I still belong to you."

She paused, her face flushed hot. If Gregory noticed her odd choice of words, he didn't react, other than to lift his brows slightly.

She knew they were true. She did belong to him somehow, even though they were two separate people. He occupied her thoughts constantly, was edging his way into her heart but had yet to make it into her bed.

Though it was wrong, she wanted him, wanted him to possess her body the way he did her mind. But she had no idea if he wanted her for more than one night.

Vanessa cleared her throat. "I meant, of course I'm still working for you, Gregory."

He smiled, but it didn't reach his eyes. "Then why are you displaying his materials?"

She shrugged, not ashamed, but indifferent. "We don't have a budget, so this is a grassroots effort. Billingsly hopped on board. He paid for this booth, and in return, he gets advertising space."

"What about me?" Gregory complained, a trace of betrayal in his voice. "After all, you are my campaign manager. You should have stacks of my post-cards here, too!"

"You hate the carousel, remember?" Vanessa shot back pleasantly.

He shook his head in disbelief. "And you think Billingsly doesn't?"

"I know his money doesn't," Vanessa quipped.

Gregory turned away, and guilt slithered through her. She touched his arm, hoping to ease the betrayal that she knew he was feeling.

"I know it's unconventional and probably a little bit wrong to have allowed Billingsly to donate the booth, but you and I have been on opposite sides about the carousel from the very beginning."

She bent her head and grasped his arm tighter so he was forced to turn and look at her. "If I'd asked you for the money, would you have given it to me?"

His eyes were dark, but she saw something else in them, too: understanding.

Yes, she'd betrayed him, but the reason was close to her heart. And when he shook his head ever so slowly, she didn't feel hurt, only sadness.

"Let me show you something."

She grabbed his hand and led him over to a small clearing next to the booth.

There she'd created a miniature art gallery of sorts, comprised of large corkboards that had been wheeled out from various classrooms at the high school. Drawings of the carousel, done by local children using crayon, markers or watercolors, were already attracting the attention of festivalgoers.

"Aren't they amazing? The carousel is special to the kids who live here. Surely it can be special in some way to you?"

Gregory sighed heavily. "Don't you ever give up?"

"Not if you won't." Vanessa smiled sweetly.

"Yoo-hoo!" Maisie called from a short distance away. "Mayor Langston, how good to see you! Where have you been hiding?"

"Under a rock, obviously. We'll talk about this later," he whispered in Vanessa's ear before quickly putting some space between them.

Maisie ambled over and pecked Vanessa on the cheek. "Hi, dear. What a terrific event!" She put her hands on her ample hips and appraised the couple. "And you make a great team. Look cute together, too, like a regular president and his first lady."

Vanessa felt her face go hot, as Gregory shifted in place next to her uncomfortably. "Maisie, would you mind the booth while I walk the mayor around the fair?"

"Absolutely. Take your time. I'll be glad to sit down under the tent and get away from this heat."

As Vanessa walked around the festival with Gregory, every so often his bare arm would brush against hers, sending a rush of sensation throughout her body.

Or he would be talking with someone and she'd feel his eyes on her as he brought her into the realm of his conversation. Whenever he did that, it was as if she was more than his campaign manager—she was his partner.

They stopped at a concession stand for lemonades, and a few booths down, there was Billingsly, shaking hands and talking loudly.

Vanessa got the odd sense that he was watching them, but she quickly put it out of her mind. She had enough to worry about without getting overly paranoid.

"He's been pretty quiet in the paper lately. What gives?" Gregory said.

"Maybe he's got nothing to talk about. After all, everything he's said about you has been a lie."

Gregory drained his lemonade and wiped his mouth. "Guys like him always find something to talk about. It's when they're quiet that you have to worry about them."

There were interrupted by a clown on stilts who reached down and handed Vanessa a business card.

"'Theodore Langston—personal injury attorney,'" she read aloud, and then handed Gregory the card.

He shook his head. "It figures. Even though his firm always has more clients and cases than they can handle, my father will do anything to keep the personal injury pipeline filled with suckers."

Gregory trotted after the stilt walker and gave him back the card. "Dude, you need this more than I do."

Vanessa caught up with him, laughing. "It sounds like you don't agree with your father's line of work."

"I don't. That's why I left and got into politics. If I don't win this election, I don't know what I'll do next."

He turned to her, a smile on his face. "Are you hiring?"

Vanessa started to loop her arm through his but quickly stopped, her gaze occupied. "No, but it looks like Ruby needs some help. Let's go check it out."

They jogged down to Ruby's booth, where a crowd was gathering.

"What's going on?" Vanessa asked.

"We've almost run out of doughnuts," Ruby said, out of breath. "I've got some more in the van, but I can't go there and be here at the same time."

"I'll go get them," Vanessa offered.

"What can I do to help?"

"I've got another huge carafe of coffee. Can you bring that, Mayor?"

"Absolutely! Where's your van parked?"

"In the teachers' parking lot, behind the school and under the tree. Door's unlocked. You can't miss it."

"We'll be as quick as we can," Vanessa promised.

They hurried across the parking lot and around the school.

When they reached the teachers' lot, Vanessa stopped to take a breath. She gazed at the redbrick building in front of her. "Bay Point High is my alma mater. This place sure brings back memories."

"Good ones, I hope," Gregory said.

She shrugged. "I made it out. That's what counts."

"Were you popular?"

"Not really. I was voted Most Likely to Disappear." She waved away Gregory's shocked expression. "The title wasn't what you think. I could never stop talking about leaving Bay Point." She laughed a little. "The ink wasn't even dry on my diploma when I did."

They continued walking to the van. "So if you were so hot to leave when you were a teenager, why did you come back?"

"I missed my parents."

That was true. Gregory didn't have to know that she had run back to the safety and security of Bay Point because she had almost lost herself for a man in Los Angeles.

Gregory had a wistful look in his eyes. "I can understand that."

He opened the back door. Vanessa reached in for the doughnuts.

"Wait," he said, touching her shoulder. "Your parents. Are they still in love?"

She turned toward him. "Yes, they are. Very much so."

He grabbed her hand and led her around to the side of the van, to where they would be hidden by the door.

"How does a love like that start?" he asked, wrapping his arms around her and pulling her close. "Does it start like this?"

Vanessa had only a second to moan yes before he lowered his lips to hers.

Chapter 13

Vanessa cast a worried glance at the door. "What time is Stodwell supposed to be here?"

Gregory checked his watch. "In about fifteen minutes. But sometimes he arrives early."

Her shoulders trembled as he slid her raincoat off, his fingertips itching to do more. Much more.

He wanted to tell her how beautiful she looked, but he held back, as he had been doing since they'd been working together. He wished it were his hands circling her waist, instead of the thin black belt adorning her short-sleeved red dress.

If things went right today, he was hopeful that he wouldn't have to hold back his feelings much longer.

Gregory turned away briefly and hung up her coat, releasing the faint scent of her perfume.

"Are you sure you want me here?" she asked, rubbing her hands up and down her bare arms.

"Positive. I left you out before. I'm not going to do that again."

He gestured to the chair in front of his desk. She shook her head and remained standing.

"Plus, I have a special announcement that I think will interest you."

Her lips hinted at a smile that teased his senses. "Let me guess—you're going to run for president?"

He laughed. "No. At least not yet, but if I did, would you consider being my first lady?"

Vanessa's eyes seemed to sparkle. "That's quite a serious question for a Monday morning."

"Mrs. Barnell said we looked good together. I just happen to agree."

Her smile widened. "Let's concentrate on winning this election first, before we move it on up to the White House."

Gregory reached for her hand. "With you at my side, I can do anything."

Her smile turned tentative, and Gregory felt a jolt of disappointment when she pulled away.

Vanessa walked to the window. "Brr. I know it's unseasonably chilly outside, but it's even colder in here."

"We've been having some problems with the air-conditioning throughout city hall." He moved to stand just behind her. "But I know a way we can turn up the heat."

Without warning, he swept her hair away from her neck and planted a kiss just behind her ear. "C'mon, Vanessa. Live dangerously."

She bent her head slightly forward, exposing more of her skin, but before he could kiss her again, she stepped out of reach.

"No, I don't want to do anything more to jeopardize your campaign," she insisted, her voice a little shaky. She walked to the front of his desk and sat down.

"What are you talking about?" he asked, sitting in the chair opposite her.

He reached for her hand. This time she didn't pull away.

She met his eyes. "I should have never let Billingsly get involved and pay for the Save the Carousel booth. Can you ever forgive me?"

"I thought my kiss at the festival proved in no uncertain terms that all was forgotten. But if I need to show you again…" His voice trailed off.

He inched his body to the edge of the chair and leaned forward to kiss her but was stopped when she put a hand on his chest.

"Need I remind you that Stodwell will be here any second?"

He stuck out his tongue. "You're no fun."

"It was wonderful. Risky, but wonderful," she admitted.

"And far too short for my liking."

She giggled. "We couldn't have stayed there

kissing all afternoon. If we hadn't brought back the doughnuts, Ruby and everyone else would have gotten suspicious!"

Gregory sank back with a groan. "A man can dream, can't he?"

Vanessa smiled sweetly and crossed her long bare legs. "And a woman still needs to hear the words."

He leaned forward and traced a circle on her knee with the tip of his finger. "Okay. I forgive you, but only if you have dinner with me tomorrow night."

She lowered her eyes and watched him. For a moment, she seemed to be lost in thought, and he wondered what she was thinking.

Was she considering the risks?

Weighing the benefits?

Fantasizing about what could possibly happen?

"I would love to."

Gregory heaved a sigh of relief as a surge of excitement coursed through his body.

Her eyes lit up. "But you have to promise me something, too."

"What's that?" he asked.

She uncrossed her legs and leaned toward him. "Keep an open mind about the carousel."

His brow furrowed. "What makes you think I don't?"

"Oh, I don't know." She pursed her lips. "That little shadow that comes over your face whenever I talk about it. Why does that happen?"

He slumped back into his chair like someone accused of a crime and said nothing.

"It's almost like you're pulling the covers over your head and trying to hide from something," Vanessa continued.

But she wasn't accusing him. Her eyes were caring, and her tone was light.

His heart warmed, because for the first time, her concern seemed to be more for him rather than her beloved carousel.

Still, he wasn't about to reveal his thoughts yet. It wasn't the right time, and he wasn't sure if that time would ever arrive.

He didn't know what Vanessa felt about him, other than the fact that she was attracted to him. Her eyes glistened whenever she looked at him, and each time he kissed her, she took longer to let him go. As if she didn't want him to stop.

As if he *wanted* to stop.

He stood up and walked over to the bookcase. "You wouldn't understand."

"I'd like to try."

He turned and blew out a breath, but his throat still felt constricted.

"Look. I'm willing to keep an open mind, just as long as you realize that I need to do what's best for the community."

Vanessa got up and stood in front of him. Something had changed in her face. The softness of it seemed harder somehow, and he knew he had hurt her.

"So do I, Gregory, and the over one thousand people who signed our petition at the festival agree with me."

She crossed her arms over her chest and he leaned an elbow on the bookshelf, appraising her and trying to think of a way to bridge the gap between them before it was too late.

It had hurt him when she'd partnered up with Billingsly. Even though he understood the reasoning behind the move, it made him want to hold back his feelings about her, be less likely to trust her.

A knock on the door interrupted their conversation.

"We'll talk about this later," he whispered.

When Vanessa nodded, Gregory went over and opened his office door.

"George! Thank you for stopping by."

The men shook hands. Stodwell placed his briefcase on the floor and shrugged out of his coat. Gregory hung it next to Vanessa's and offered the man some coffee.

He declined. "I hope you have good news for me, Mayor."

"You know my campaign manager, Vanessa Hamilton, don't you?"

Stodwell narrowed his eyes, as if he didn't recognize her, but then his face changed to one of embarrassment. "Of course—she's one of my tenants," he blustered. "How are you?"

Vanessa nodded her greeting but said nothing more.

"Shall we all have a seat?"

Gregory gestured to a small conference table on one side of his office. The trio walked over and sat down.

"Mr. Stodwell, I know you're a busy man, and I don't want to waste your time, so I'll get right to it. I've met with city council, and they have agreed to purchase your commercial buildings."

Stodwell's eyes widened, and Gregory could almost see the dollar signs.

"That's terrific!" Stodwell exclaimed.

Gregory held up his hand to quell the man's excitement. "However, we are only willing to pay one percent over your asking price, and our offer is contingent upon the satisfactory outcome of all the inspections by our buildings department."

"I'm sure they'll all pass with flying colors."

"Are you kidding me?" Vanessa said. "I've had a leak in my storage room for over six months."

Stodwell scratched his chin. "I thought I sent someone out to fix that a long time ago."

Vanessa crossed her arms. "That's what you told Lucy and a number of other business owners downtown, too. Each one has something different that is wrong. The only thing we all have in common is that it never gets fixed!"

"Am I on trial here?" he blasted back, opening his arms wide in offense. "Why is she here, anyway, Mayor?"

He caught her eyes, but he quickly looked away, focusing on the man next to him.

"Vanessa is an important part of my campaign team. She is here as a witness to our discussions, not only as one of your tenants but also as a member of the community."

"Your mother, she's an activist, right?"

"She is," Vanessa acknowledged. "So what?"

"So how do you think she's going to feel about the local government owning the building that houses your small business?"

Gregory didn't like the man's tone, and from what he heard, neither did Vanessa.

"Blooms in Paradise is my flower shop, not my mother's."

She stared at the men in front of her, her eyes hard and unyielding, and Gregory knew that whatever she was about to say was meant for both of them.

"If I could, I'd buy the building myself. But since I can't, I'd want to make sure that the city would make the proper repairs so that I can concentrate on running my business, rather than worrying about all the stuff I can't afford to fix myself."

A reddish tint spread over Stodwell's chubby cheeks. "I can get a lot more money if I sell my properties to the developers outright."

Gregory leaned back in his chair. He'd known Stodwell was going to bring up that point, and he was ready for him.

"You could. But you won't get out of the inspection process. In fact, it'll take longer. I've already talked to them. As you know, they buy and sell properties all over the United States. The backlog of inspections for current properties they're interested in purchasing is twelve months."

"That's an entire year!" Stodwell thundered.

"On the other hand, if you deal with us, we can get those inspections done in no more than sixty days, which puts you a lot closer to that extended golf vacation in Hawaii."

While Stodwell puffed out his cheeks and looked defeated, Gregory swiveled his attention to Vanessa.

"And just to put your mind at ease, city council and I have already allocated monies within the redevelopment budget to cover the cost of the purchase of the buildings and necessary repairs.

"If I am reelected," he continued, "I'm going to create a tenant association for downtown business owners and will recommend that you lead the group."

Vanessa gave him a wary smile, and he couldn't tell if she was upset with his statements or pleased.

"Well, Mr. Stodwell?" Gregory folded his hands on the table and steepled his fingers. "Are there visions of retirement dancing in your head? Do we have a deal?"

Stodwell shifted his glance toward Gregory and held it, and he shook his head. "I must be getting soft in my old age. Either that, or I've had too many dreams about hot women in hula skirts, but yeah, you've got a deal."

Gregory stood, hoping the man would take the hint. Vanessa was being awfully quiet, and he wanted to be sure that she was okay.

"Terrific." He made a show of looking at his watch. "I've got another meeting in a few minutes. I'll have my assistant contact you within the next few days to discuss the inspection process, and our attorney will begin to draw up the papers."

Stodwell grabbed his coat and slung it over his arm. "Oh, I almost forgot."

He opened his briefcase, pulled out the *Bay Point Courier*, folded it and handed it to Gregory.

"Be careful of the company you keep. You never know when someone's going to stab you in the back."

Gregory waited till he left, and then he brought the paper over to the conference table and unfolded it to the front page.

On it there was one picture of Jacob Billingsly with his arm casually slung around Vanessa's shoulders, a pose similar to what Gregory had seen him do at the community festival.

Next to it was a picture of Vanessa and Gregory. It appeared to be taken at the town hall meeting, but the pose made it seem as if they were at odds with each other, which was completely untrue.

The headline above the pictures read Abandon Ship?

Vanessa covered her mouth and gasped. "I'm so sorry, Gregory. I thought that maybe since Jacob contributed to the carousel, he'd stop harassing you. This is all my fault."

"We both know what he's capable of, and that he's been quiet the last week or so. It was only a matter of time."

Gregory's eyes slid shut for a moment. When he opened them, he glanced back at the door.

"I'm not entirely sure Jacob was responsible for this."

Nor was he sure whom in Bay Point he could trust anymore, including the beautiful woman standing beside him.

Chapter 14

There's something about being in a stretch limo that can make an ordinary day seem like Christmas, Vanessa thought as she snuggled her back against the black leather seat.

When Gregory had asked her to dinner, he hadn't mentioned it would be at the Langstons' beachfront estate. And he'd insisted on sending his father's part-time chauffeur to pick her up. She'd put up a fuss—for about two minutes—and then given in.

She helped herself to a small bottle of ice-cold mineral water from the minibar. "Might as well enjoy it."

The chauffeur glanced at her through the rear-view mirror.

"Don't tell your boss!" she instructed.

He grinned, nodded and slid the privacy window closed.

After a long swallow, she opened her compact. The hint of makeup she'd applied earlier was still intact. That afternoon several orders had come through her website, and it had taken the rest of the day to fill them. She'd had just enough time to change her clothes.

It seemed only moments later when she felt a warm breeze hit her bare legs. Opening her eyes, she realized that she'd drifted off to sleep. They'd arrived, and the driver was outside waiting patiently for her to disembark from the vehicle.

She stuffed her compact in her purse. "That's some strong water you've got there," she muttered.

The driver bowed slightly with a bemused smile, as if he didn't quite get the joke, and closed the door behind her.

Her jaw dropped as she stared at the Langston estate. The rumors around town were true. It was breathtaking.

Located on a cliff overlooking the Pacific Ocean, the Spanish-style estate made of cream-colored stucco seemed to glow against the backdrop of the setting sun. A bank of windows on the first floor extended all the way to the ceiling, each framed by plantation shutters. She could only imagine the fantastic views from the wrought-iron balcony that wrapped around the entire second floor.

She was on her way up to the front door when

she heard Gregory call out, "Just follow the redbrick walkway past the front door and around. I'd come and get you, but I'm manning the grill."

He cooks? she thought as she clutched her bag and walked in the direction he'd instructed.

The tantalizing smell of barbecue chicken reached her nose even before she turned the corner. She inhaled deeply, a little too deeply, and then she saw who was waiting on the patio.

What were they all doing here?

Vanessa began to cough, deep gulping breaths, at seeing the entire Langston family.

Though she had tears in her eyes, she could see a bright yellow pantsuit hurrying toward her.

"Are you okay?" Gregory's mother asked. Her voice had a strident quality that could never calm but only induce more panic.

"I've got her, Mama," said Gregory, taking over. His warm hand gripped her arm. "Can you get Vanessa a glass of water?"

"Micah, man the barbecue, please."

Vanessa felt herself being guided by Gregory, but her eyes were watering so badly that she could barely see.

Moments later he pushed her gently down onto a lounge chair. Mrs. Langston shoved a glass of water at her, and Vanessa drank deeply. After a few more sputters, she had gained control of herself, enough to stop coughing.

Gregory's hands were on her shoulders, massaging, kneading, making her skin come alive.

Even though she was feeling better, she coughed a few more times just so he wouldn't stop.

"More water?" Mrs. Langston asked, waving the half-empty glass in front of her face.

More Gregory, she thought as she shook her head.

Gregory removed his hands and knelt by her side.

"Are you sure you're all right?"

His eyes were kind, concerned and, Vanessa dared to hope, almost loving.

"I'm okay. Thank you."

He stood and helped her to her feet. "I'd like to introduce Vanessa Hamilton, my dinner partner for this evening."

Vanessa gave an embarrassed wave. "Hi, everyone. Sorry for the less-than-grand entrance."

Gregory's mother was still close by. "Helen Langston."

Her handshake felt cool and distant.

"You've grown up into a beautiful young woman, Vanessa. I remember you as a child. Gregory could never stop talking about the little girl who loved to play with dirt. He was quite taken with you."

She looked Vanessa up and down, as if she was evaluating her on some kind of invisible rating scale, perhaps even calculating if she was good enough for her son.

"But he was only a boy then," Helen declared, as if that were the deciding factor. Vanessa didn't like the hint of superiority in her tone, and she knew that she'd failed the test.

Gregory either didn't notice or didn't care about his mother's opinion. He turned toward Vanessa, his eyes sparkling with mischief. "All it took was one playdate."

Her heart lifted in her chest. He seemed to be referring to more than just an innocent childhood outing, and she wondered if it had anything to do with tonight's surprise dinner with his family.

"Time to grow up, little bro. I'm Marlon, and though I'm a bit older than Gregory, I'm a lot more fun."

Marlon was built like a linebacker, and she felt herself being swept up into a bear hug. But Gregory quickly tugged her loose and pointed in the direction of the enormous grill.

Micah waved the barbecue tongs distractedly. "I'm Micah, and I cook better than Gregory!"

"At least my younger brother is telling the truth," Gregory informed her.

"Let the woman alone," thundered Theodore Langston good-naturedly as he strode across the stone patio. "As long as Vanessa helps Gregory win the election, she's family."

"No pressure, right?" Vanessa joked, as his father put his arm around Vanessa's shoulders and squeezed.

Everyone laughed, though Helen's sounded forced.

"The food is almost done, so why don't we all have a seat?" she said.

Gregory directed Vanessa to a large oval patio table. One end was laden with corn on the cob, pasta salad and other picnic foods. She was glad to see that the food was not served on silver platters but normal everyday plasticware. She was already uncomfortable enough without having to worry about breaking something.

Micah brought over a large tray filled with chicken. When he set it down on the table, he almost bumped his head on the red umbrella. Vanessa realized he was slightly taller than Gregory, while Marlon was a bit shorter and more powerfully built.

Gregory leaned over and whispered in Vanessa's ear, "I'll fix you a plate—what would you like?"

She shivered at the caress of his voice and the kindness of his gesture.

When they had all sat down to eat, Vanessa noticed that nobody prayed over the meal. In her family, somebody always did.

Theo Langston tucked his napkin into the collar of his shirt. "The election is next week. How's the campaign coming along?"

Gregory took a bite of chicken and swallowed. "I'm feeling pretty confident." He squeezed her hand briefly. "Vanessa has done a great job of helping me manage the public's expectations of my vision for Bay Point."

He gave her a grateful smile, and she knew he meant every word.

Vanessa wiped her mouth. "The town hall meeting helped everyone see the potential benefits of the downtown redevelopment plan."

Helen sipped her lemonade. "I think that's wonderful."

Then why didn't you show up? Why didn't any of you show up?

Vanessa sighed inwardly, realizing that other than herself and Gregory, none of the people at the table had been at the meeting. She guessed wealth bought more than waterfront homes and designer clothes; it bought apathy.

"The people had a voice and a place to vent. That's important because some folks in this town can be tougher to convince than a grand jury," Theo said, a trace of bitterness in his voice.

"Most of my father's clients aren't in Bay Point but from surrounding cities," Gregory explained. "It riles him a little bit."

Theo waved his fork in the air. "Hrumph."

Helen gestured to the Langstons' home and gardens. "Do you think we'd have all this if you had just put up your shingle in Bay Point?"

Marlon munched on some corn and swallowed. "Everyone in town knows that Micah prefers briefs over boxers. Can you blame them if they don't want to risk having the details of their lawsuits spilling over into the party lines?"

"Most people in Bay Point are too smart to get involved with an ambulance chaser," Micah said from the grill, where he was plating the rest of the meat.

"He's a personal injury attorney," Helen told Vanessa, who didn't have the heart to tell her that she already knew that little fact.

When her son walked over and offered her more chicken, Helen shook her head in disapproval. "You know how your father hates that term."

"And it's a ridiculous one at that," Gregory said, rushing to his father's defense. "Dad couldn't chase a dog, let alone an ambulance."

Theodore Langston patted his ample belly and laughed. "If I did, I might end up having to represent myself."

Everyone chuckled but without warmth.

Vanessa shifted in her seat uncomfortably. She was used to the good-natured ribbing that went along with having one brother and two parents who clearly loved each other.

When she was a child, she treasured the times her family was together all at once. Since her father was often at the hospital, those gatherings were all very special. Sure, they had moments when she and her brother, Charlie, would argue, but for the most part, the Hamilton family was happy and content.

On the other hand, there seemed to be an undercurrent of hostility within the Langston family, and she wondered why it was there. The dynamic was strange and different, and she was unsure how to react.

Theo downed his second lemonade and set his glass on the table. "Well, Gregory, if you don't win, you can always come back and work for me."

"That'll never happen," Gregory vowed. "I'll win, Dad."

Theo shook his head but said nothing further. Everyone resumed eating, and nobody seemed to want to challenge the two men.

"When Gregory does win, he's going to take a victory ride on the Bay Point Carousel," Vanessa teased, hoping to break the tension around the table.

"That old rattletrap?" Theo grunted a harsh laugh. "You ride that thing, son, and you might need my services after all."

"Let him alone, Theo," Helen admonished. "You never took him to ride it as a kid, so now he has a second chance."

Vanessa glanced over at Gregory. His jaw was clenched, and he appeared poised to make a fast getaway. Suddenly she knew why he hated the carousel so much.

He threw his napkin down on the table. "Don't worry, Dad," he said, his voice tinged with anger. "It doesn't even work anymore."

"Then it's a good thing you're tearing it down," Theo said. "It serves no purpose and is taking up valuable space."

"I never thought I'd see the day when you two

would agree on something. Must be the chicken," Marlon quipped before piling more meat on his plate.

Micah, an aspiring chef, said, "Good food can always bring families together."

Gregory stood abruptly. "Not this one. Vanessa, are you finished eating?" he asked.

She nodded, even though she really wasn't, and placed her fork on her half-filled plate.

"Good, because I've suddenly lost my appetite." He held out his hand, and she took it.

"Let's go down to the beach."

As he led her away, Vanessa knew that no one would argue, and no one would come after them.

Chapter 15

When they reached the Langstons' private beach, they removed their shoes and left them at the bottom of the wooden stairs.

"What's going to happen now?" Vanessa asked.

Gregory lifted his chin toward the cliff. "They'll finish the meal in silence, and they'll all go their separate ways, like always."

I don't care anymore, he silently vowed, but he knew that he did.

He made his way to a small cabana, opened the door and grabbed a blanket. She followed him the short distance to the shore, where he spread the blanket and they both sat down.

The sun was beginning to sink down into the horizon, casting a warm orange glow on the waters of the Pacific.

He wrapped his arms around his knees. "I'm sorry I interrupted your dinner, but I had to get away from there."

She faced him, sitting cross-legged. "No, it was my fault. I should have never mentioned the carousel."

"You didn't know what my reaction would be."

"That's right, Gregory. I didn't know."

She laid her hand on his arm, and the muscle beneath twitched under her fingers. "Why didn't you ever tell me the reason why you don't like the carousel?"

"It's not that I don't like it," he said defensively.

"Then why don't you tell me the real reason why you're against it," she corrected.

He couldn't look at her, didn't want to see the hope in her eyes, so he stared at the waves rolling onto the sand.

"Because carousels and merry-go-rounds are totally false. The horses, the lights, even the music are designed to draw kids, and even adults, into a lie. It's wrong, Vanessa."

"What do you mean? What kind of lie?"

"The lie that if you ride it, you and your family will be happy."

"Are you saying that your father never took you on the carousel because he didn't want you to be happy?"

He turned toward her. "Hard to believe, right? But it's true."

When she didn't comment, he rose from the blanket and walked a few feet away. He stood at the edge of the shore, where the waves just barely reached his feet, wishing that he'd never said anything.

Vanessa got up and caught up to him. "Maybe he had another reason. Maybe he truly believed it wasn't safe."

"And maybe he just didn't have the time." He turned around, shoved his hands in the pockets of his trousers. "Maybe neither of them did."

She stroked her hands down his arms. Her touch was like fire, and she tugged his hands into hers.

"I'm sorry, Gregory. I guess I'm like most people in that I thought that because your parents were wealthy, you didn't have any problems."

Vanessa stood before him, trying to draw him out of himself as easily as she'd drawn his hands out of his pockets. He already knew that she cared about his campaign, but maybe she even cared about him.

"We did have problems. I guess we still do," he muttered, trying to see past his pain to the opportunity he had with Vanessa.

"But it's too late. We've all gone our separate ways. Micah is in culinary school. Marlon's an engineer. I'm a politician. My mom still works on behalf of various lobbyists on Capitol Hill, and my dad is still chasing ambulances."

His heart constricted in his chest as he realized

the only thing the members of his family had in common was that they all shared the same last name and a talent for making money.

Vanessa threw her arms around his neck, surprising him. He pulled her close and bent his head so he could smell the clean fragrance of her hair.

"It's never too late," she insisted. "You can't erase the past, but you can create something new."

He wanted so much to believe her. His family, particularly his father, had been a source of hurt and frustration for so long. Though he'd grown up with every privilege a child could want, all he'd really wanted was for his family to be normal. To pray together, stay together and, most of all, be together.

But that had rarely happened, and now that everyone was all grown up, he doubted that it ever would.

With Vanessa in his arms, he could forget about everything, except how much he wanted her.

"Remember the last time we were on the beach?"

She leaned away from him, looked in his eyes and nodded.

"All evening I've been trying to ignore how beautiful you look in your pale pink sundress. Sweetheart neckline. Very modest." He traced his finger across her collarbone. "In my opinion, this dress is even sexier than the one you had on last time."

"The one I got wet saving your hat from the ocean?"

He nodded and pulled her close again. "Can you

save me now? Not the election. Not the carousel. Not my hat. Just me."

Her lithe body felt so right in his arms, and when her eyes slid shut, he kissed her. That felt right, too.

The waves crashed around their feet, but it didn't compare to the roaring in his ears when Vanessa opened her mouth a little wider. His tongue slipped in, darting and exploring where it hadn't before, dueling with hers as she clung to him.

She slid her hands up and down his back and then under his shirt, pleasing him with her boldness. Without breaking his kiss, he reached between them and quickly undid his buttons. She pushed his shirt off his shoulders. It got caught in a wave and swept off to sea.

Vanessa traced her hands over his chest, drawing circles with her tongue in his mouth. She seemed to want to consume him, and he was happy to oblige.

He positioned his hands around her bottom, kneading and cupping her curves, before he gently picked her up.

Vanessa wrapped her legs around his waist, and he could feel her heat against his lower abdomen.

He pulsed against her, already hard as a rock and getting harder by the second, as she slowly moved up and down against him, moaning into his ear.

With his lips on hers, he carried her up the beach, having to guess where the blanket was because he didn't want to stop kissing her. He didn't mind if he walked around aimlessly holding her against him as long as he could feel her sweet lips upon his.

Moments later his toes brushed soft cotton and he laid her down gently. Her dress was up around her waist, exposing her white lace underwear. She reached around to the back of her dress, trying to undo the zipper. Kneeling at her side, he beat her to it and helped her remove her dress from her body.

"Vanessa," he breathed, in awe of her body, now clad only in her lace bra and panties, and what they were about to do. "Are you sure?"

She didn't say a word. Instead she turned on her side, nodded and reached for his belt buckle. Still kneeling, he let her unfasten and slide it from his trousers. Then her hand stroked him outside of his pants, and he groaned before she slid down his zipper. He stood up and stepped out of his pants and knelt back down again. When her hand immediately went inside his briefs, exposing his flesh, he wasted no time in removing them, too.

Gregory knelt at Vanessa's side a third time and spread his legs a little. She knelt in front of him, and his penis arrowed forth against her mouth. When she licked him the first time, he plunged his hands in her hair, until she gradually licked down and took his entire length in her mouth.

He groaned aloud while she pumped her mouth against him, her tongue ever circling his thickness, ever sucking at the core. Her nose, at times, became buried in his hair. Her hands gently kneaded his buttocks until he felt he was going to burst from the pleasure.

He withdrew. He had to, or else he would have come, and he wanted more for her than just his pleasure. He wanted to feel her and know that she was his.

Gregory lay on the blanket, and Vanessa straddled him. She popped off her bra, exposing the breasts that had been the subject of many of his dreams.

With her nipples she teased him, rubbing them lightly over his chest. They felt like sparks against his skin, hot and electric. When she leaned over and dangled her breasts in front of his mouth, he indulged. Rubbing his hands down her spine, he sucked and sucked, and she squirmed and ground her heat against him, until her juices soaked through her underwear onto his hot skin.

"Enough!" he breathed against her wet breast. Still, he couldn't help laving her nipple with his tongue as he used both hands to tear the panties from her body.

She lifted up her torso, put one hand on his chest and positioned the tip of his penis outside of her body. She rubbed against him, teasing him over and over with her slick, wet folds.

Gregory gritted his teeth and lifted his buttocks toward heaven, and she slid him inside. At the core of his being and in the center of her innermost heat, they rocked together, faster than the waves yet still trying to control themselves in that mind grip of inescapable pleasure, until finally Vanessa reached the point of no return.

"Never enough," she cried out, through gasps of hot breaths in his ear. Beautiful, sensuous sounds he knew he'd never want to forget and that he needed to hear again.

"Never enough," he whispered back, still thrusting milk-white heat into her body. "I couldn't agree more."

Chapter 16

Vanessa closed and locked the door to Blooms in Paradise and then tugged on Gregory's hand, trying to hurry him along down the sidewalk. She and the committee had worked most of the weekend on sprucing up the carousel, and tonight was the big reveal.

It was also the night before the mayoral election.

Luckily, Gregory had been out of town with his mother in Washington, DC, so he hadn't been anywhere near downtown for the past few days.

She was flattered that as soon as he arrived back in Bay Point, he'd come straight to the flower shop, but she could tell that he wasn't in the best of moods. But he'd barely stepped over the threshold when she'd closed the shop for the evening and practically pushed him out the door.

"What's the big rush, Vanessa? You know tomorrow is the election. We're supposed to be working on my victory speech."

"I told you, that's exactly what we're going to do once we get to Ruby's," she lied, hoping that he wouldn't remember that the pastry shop always closed early on Monday nights.

It was dark outside, but he made sure no one was watching before he suddenly stopped in front of the doorway of the abandoned hardware store.

"I've missed you," he said thickly, pulling her into his arms. "I'd rather work on the speech at your place."

The kiss he gave her then was deep and bursting with so much passion that she nearly turned around and headed back to her apartment.

She broke the kiss, arriving back at her senses for now.

But she knew that tonight was too important, not only to Bay Point's future but to hers and Gregory's.

"Then we wouldn't get anything done," she replied, ignoring Gregory's playful scowl. "Let's go, before we're too late."

When they arrived at city hall, Vanessa reached into her purse and retrieved her cell phone. He hadn't said anything about the carousel, and for once, she was glad.

"What are we doing here?" Gregory asked, watching her suspiciously as she sent a text message. "I thought we were going to Ruby's."

"Turn around," Vanessa commanded, her eyes alert and watchful. She didn't want him to see what was going to happen next. Not yet.

"Why? What's going on?"

"Turn around and trust me." She grasped both of his hands and looked deep into his eyes. "I need you to do that for me."

Reluctantly, Gregory turned around. She breathed a sigh of relief, then immediately held her breath and crossed her fingers, hoping that everything would go exactly as she planned.

"What are you going to do, Vanessa? Arrest me?" he joked, crossing his hands behind his back. "Because the only thing I'm guilty of is—"

His words were cut off by the sound of gears creaking and turning.

He whirled around to see the carousel, like a gentle giant, slowly come back to life after a long and deep slumber. A rainbow of lights blinked on, the horses began to go up and down in perfect concert with the organ groove.

The shocked look on Gregory's face was as priceless as the surprise itself.

"What in the world?" His eyes widened with amazement. "You got it working?"

She nodded, then stopped. "Well, not really me personally. Prentice played a huge role. He knew someone who could fix the carousel enough so you could see that it still works."

She took his hand. "Come on—let's go for a ride."

He stopped in his tracks and refused to budge. "I think I'd rather be arrested."

Vanessa laughed and pulled on his hand again. "I'll put you in handcuffs later. But right now there's a horse over there with your name on it."

She unhitched the door of the rusty iron gate that surrounded the carousel. When they had walked through, she closed and latched the gate.

"Wait here."

She quickly walked the inside perimeter. Prentice had started the carousel for her and, as requested, had disappeared from sight.

Although this was supposed to be a private viewing for the mayor only, it was just a matter of time before someone stopped by, wondering what all the fuss was about.

Plus, earlier that day the man who'd fixed the carousel had warned her that he wasn't sure how long it would work. More parts were needed, as well as more time to make it not only run well but also run consistently.

Vanessa was hoping it would take only one ride to convince Gregory not to demolish the carousel.

She hurried back to him. "So did you pick out your horse?"

He shook his head. "It's tough to choose. They all look almost brand-new. What did you do to them?"

Vanessa smiled, pleased that he had noticed. "We actually didn't have time to paint all the horses, so we just painted the saddles and the poles."

"They look fantastic. Is the paint dry? I don't want to walk around town with a golden butt."

She laughed. "I think so, but we can always sit on the lovers' bench instead."

He put his arm around her waist and squeezed. "That sounds perfect for us."

Normally, the carousel would be stopped and then people would get on. That was normal, safe operating procedure.

"Aren't you, or whoever is running this thing, going to stop it so we can get on safely?"

"That's normal operating procedure," Vanessa replied. "But I'm not sure how long it's going to be running. The mechanic told me it needs more parts to make it run really well."

"Sounds like you and I are going to have to jump on," Gregory said. "Are you up for that?"

She flashed him a confident smile and grabbed his hand. "It's running at a snail's pace. We can handle it."

There was the slightest breeze from its slow-as-molasses rotation, but it was not even enough to lift Vanessa's hair from her shoulders.

Gregory grabbed one of the freestanding poles lining the outside perimeter and hopped on first. The carousel went around once, and then Vanessa reached for Gregory's hand and he helped her up.

They dodged the horses that were rising up and down until they reached the lovers' bench.

"So what do you think?"

"I think it looks phenomenal," Gregory admitted. "How many people did you have working on it?"

"About twenty-five each day. Even Billingsly stopped by."

He jerked his chin at her. "He did? What did he do?"

"Passed out literature, mostly. When he finally figured out that no one was really interested, he left."

She put her hand on his knee. "I don't think you have to worry about Jacob anymore. His days in Bay Point are numbered, and tomorrow's election will prove it."

"I appreciate the vote of confidence." Gregory gazed into her eyes. "But I do need to worry about you."

She tilted her head. "What do you mean?"

"You've put your heart and soul into getting the carousel working. I don't want my decision on whether to demolish it or not to affect us.

"Will it?" His eyes searched hers. "What's wrong?"

Her heart fell. "I guess I thought that just showing you that the carousel still worked would be enough to change your mind."

He squeezed her hand. "Several weeks ago, I wouldn't have even stepped foot inside the gate, and regardless of whether the carousel was fixed or not, I was pretty set in my attitude about it.

"Now that you know my secret, the fact that I wanted to ride the carousel as a child but was never given the opportunity, I feel like I need to take some time to decide."

He didn't say no, she thought. *There's still hope.*

She smiled. "All I'm asking is that you think about it. Think about all the joy that the carousel can still bring to Bay Point, and even to you, if you'd keep an open mind."

"I'll render my decision a few days after the election, okay?"

Vanessa nodded, grateful that he was going to thoughtfully consider the future of the carousel. All she could do now was wait and pray.

Chapter 17

The next morning, Vanessa got up early to vote and then decided to visit Mrs. Barnell to see if she needed a ride to the polling station. Maisie neither owned a car nor drove and relied completely upon her friends for transportation.

When Vanessa arrived, she rapped loudly on the back door. It was cracked open a bit, but her elderly friend was nowhere in sight.

She put down the vase that held Maisie's daily bouquet of flowers on the stone patio. The small parking lot in back of Maisie's bed-and-breakfast was empty of cars. Either she'd had no guests the previous night, or they had already checked out.

"Maisie, are you in there?" she called out loudly,

without a trace of panic, yet her voice seemed muted under the canopy of trees that graced the patio.

No answer.

As far as she knew, Maisie could hear just fine. Something was wrong.

Worry trickled through her as Vanessa flattened her palm against the polished wood. The door swung open.

"Mrs. Barnell?" she called out again. She picked up the vase of flowers and lightly brushed her hip against the door. It closed with a soft click that strangely amplified her sense of worry.

Still carrying the vase, she held her breath as she made her way through the '50s-era-style kitchen, the only part of Maisie's home that had not been updated when it had been converted into a bed-and-breakfast.

Vanessa found her friend sitting in the front parlor in her favorite armchair. One veined hand was resting loosely on her lap, and the other held a photo, which Vanessa knew was of her late husband.

She almost cried with relief, and she buried her nose in the fragrant mix of freesia and pale pink roses so that Mrs. Barnell wouldn't see.

But she needn't have been concerned. Maisie didn't acknowledge Vanessa, though she had to know she was in the room. Without looking at her, she merely spoke in a quiet voice.

"Today would have been our fiftieth wedding anniversary."

Her eyes smarted again at the pensive quality in

Maisie's tone. There was a trace of hope cast amid the doom of finality. It had been only what, two, maybe three, years since her husband had passed, Vanessa thought. The woman was still grieving. She had a right to reflect on what might have been.

"Well, then, I'm glad I brought you your daily bouquet. Today is a day that should be celebrated."

Maisie finally turned her face toward Vanessa. There were tears in her eyes, but a faint smile crossed her lips.

"You know, you're right." She paused to hug the photo to her chest. "It's a day to celebrate an unlikely beginning."

Vanessa raised a brow and walked up to her. She set the vase down on the table next to Maisie. "What do you mean?"

"When I first met Frank, my late husband, I didn't like him at all," she confessed.

It was then that Vanessa noticed that Maisie was still in her bathrobe. Concern filled her. Was she ill?

She peered at Maisie as best she could without being intrusive, but other than red-rimmed eyes and the late-day pajamas, there was nothing else out of the ordinary about her friend.

"We met, and eventually fell in love, at the Bay Point Carousel. Lots of people have experienced the same thing. There's something magical about it."

She lifted her eyes and stared at Vanessa. "You have to save the carousel."

"I'm trying. I brought Gregory—" she cleared her

throat "—I mean the mayor, and showed him that it's working. He said he'd think about it and let me know after the election."

Maisie nodded. "The carousel brought me and my husband together. It'll do the same for you and Gregory."

Vanessa shook her head. "There's nothing going on between us."

"For once, I'm going to have to believe what the rumor mill says, but only because your eyes light up whenever you mention the mayor's name."

Vanessa grinned. "Am I that obvious?"

"True love isn't easy to hide."

Maisie gently placed the picture of her late husband on the end table next to her. "How does he feel about you?"

"I'm not sure." She shrugged. "He did ask me if his decision about the carousel would affect our relationship."

"Would it?" Maisie asked.

Vanessa sank down on the opposite chair. "I don't know. I don't even want to think about what would happen if he decides to go ahead with the demolition."

The two women sat in silence for a while as the grandfather clock in the hallway ticked time away. When it began to chime, Maisie stood up.

"Will you drive me to the polling station over at the high school, Vanessa? I've got something that might change Gregory's mind."

Chapter 18

Gregory sat on the lovers' bench of the carousel, waiting for Vanessa. The days since winning the election by a landslide had been a flurry of activity. Although Vanessa had attended his victory celebration at the high school, she'd been noticeably distant. He hoped tonight would change all of that.

He checked his phone for a message from Vanessa. It was nearly ten o'clock in the evening, and the streets were deserted. That would change soon, too. Now that he had been reelected to a second term, he could begin to take action on the redevelopment plan.

The only light came from the soft glow of the old-fashioned streetlamps that dotted the perimeter of the square. The carousel was dormant again, the horses frozen in time. He heard the click of the gate and soft footsteps on the pavement. And suddenly she was there.

"Hello." There was a slight tremble in her voice, and he knew it was his fault.

Though she was dressed in jeans and a white V-neck sweater, she rubbed her hands up and down her arms as if she was cold.

Gregory stood and extended his hand. "I'll help you up."

Her palms were cool to the touch, and he kept her hand in his when they sat down on the lovers' bench.

Silence stretched between them. She was scared about what he was going to say. He was scared about her reaction.

The crickets let them know they were not alone.

"Peaceful out here, isn't it?" Vanessa said.

Gregory nodded. "I wish I hadn't been so stubborn about the carousel for so long. It's a great place to just think."

She turned to him. "What were you thinking about?"

"The election. Winning a second term is humbling, but there's a lot of work to do." He paused. "I never got a chance to thank you."

Vanessa slipped her hand from his and placed it in her lap. "You don't need to thank me, Gregory. You worked very hard during the campaign, and you deserved to win."

"We worked very hard," he corrected. "If it hadn't

been for you, it would have been me slinking out of town instead of Jacob Billingsly."

Her lips turned up into a smile. "I know we didn't think this at the time, but there's no way he would have won. He was an outsider who tried to bully his way into the office. But what he forgot was that people in Bay Point are loyal to their own, despite a difference in opinion."

"You're talking about the redevelopment plan."

Vanessa nodded. "The town hall meeting helped to sway people's opinions in our favor, but some people still don't like it. They don't like change."

"Then why didn't they show it and vote for Billingsly?"

She sat back against the bench. "I'm sure some did, but the sheer number of votes for you means that they didn't let their opinion about downtown redevelopment sway their opinion of you."

Vanessa turned toward him, her eyes shining. "You're the best man for the job, and everyone knows it."

"But am I the best man for you?"

He reached out and touched her hair. Her eyes slid shut and he kissed her gently, then moved away.

Her eyes fluttered open. "I believe that you are. I truly do, but you have to realize that my opinions about the carousel will never change. It will always divide us."

He put his arm around her and pulled her close.

"It doesn't have to divide us. Maybe it can bring us closer together."

Vanessa hitched in a breath, turned and looked up at him. "What are you saying, Gregory?"

"I've decided not to tear down the carousel."

Vanessa squealed and threw her arms around his neck. "Oh, thank you, Gregory, thank you!"

"At least not permanently," he finished, extracting himself from her grip.

"I don't understand."

"I've talked with the architect and reviewed the blueprints. We are going to adjust the plans so that the carousel will be housed within the new municipal complex. It will be dismantled and reassembled as part of the construction project."

"That's terrific!" Vanessa said. "But I thought you didn't have any money in the budget."

"And we still don't."

"If there's no money in the budget, then how is this all going to happen, Gregory? You can't raise taxes to pay for it. With the economy the way it is, people can barely afford the taxes we have in place now."

He touched a finger to her lips. "Don't worry. Somebody has made a very generous donation that will pay for everything."

Her eyes widened. "Everything?"

Gregory nodded. "Dismantling, reassembling, repair and complete restoration."

"How long will that take?"

"I've already talked to a few companies that specialize in restoring carousels. It could take as much as two years for everything to be done."

"But that's right about when the new municipal complex is slated to open, so it's perfect timing," Vanessa said with a smile.

She wrapped her arms around his neck once again and kissed him. "I'm so happy I could scream."

"Don't scream. You'll scare the crickets."

Vanessa laughed. "Who is the generous donor?"

"I thought you'd never ask. She told me she wanted to remain anonymous but said that I could tell you."

She placed her hands over her mouth in shock. "Maisie Barnell?"

"How did you guess?"

She grabbed his hands. "I went over to her house on election day, and just before I drove her to the polls, she told me that she had a way that might help change your mind about the carousel."

"A dollar sign and a lot of zeros made the decision a no-brainer," Gregory replied, grinning. "Maisie said that the carousel was a place of new beginnings that had to be preserved for future generations. Do you know what she meant?"

She nodded. "When I visited her, she told me that she and her husband fell in love sitting on this very bench. Apparently, lots of other people in town have, too."

"What about you? Have you fallen in love? I know

I have." Gregory tenderly caressed her cheek as she gazed into his eyes. "I love you, Vanessa."

She cupped his chin and drew his lips to hers. "I love you, too, Mr. Mayor."

"Ready to go on the ride of a lifetime?"

She nodded, and his heart nearly burst with happiness. He drew her into his arms, and this time he wasn't letting her go.

* * * * *

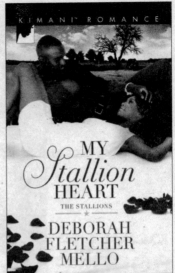

Let love in…

Beautiful Surrender

Sherelle Green

Mya Winters is organizing a charity date auction. There's one hitch: her cohost, private investigator Malik Madden, only has eyes for her. If she'd just confide in him, he could help piece together the truth about her past. But trust works both ways. And his only chance at a future with her is to share a secret that threatens their passionate connection…

An Elite Event

Available May 2015!

HARLEQUIN®
www.Harlequin.com

KPSG4030515

REQUEST YOUR FREE BOOKS!

2 FREE NOVELS
PLUS 2 FREE GIFTS!

KIMANI™
ROMANCE

Love's ultimate destination!

The first two stories in the *Love in the Limelight* series, where four unstoppable women find fame, fortune and ultimately… true love.

LOVE IN THE LIMELIGHT

New York Times bestselling author

BRENDA JACKSON

&

A.C. ARTHUR

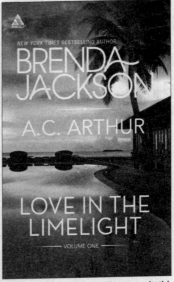

In *Star of His Heart*, Ethan Chambers is Hollywood's most eligible bachelor. But when he meets his costar Rachel Wellesley, he suddenly finds himself thinking twice about staying single.

In *Sing Your Pleasure*, Charlene Quinn has just landed a major contract with L.A.'s hottest record label, working with none other than Akil Hutton. Despite his gruff attitude, she finds herself powerfully attracted to the driven music producer.

Available now wherever books are sold!

www.Harlequin.com

The last two
stories in the
Love in the Limelight
series, where four
unstoppable women
find fame, fortune and
ultimately…true love

LOVE IN THE LIMELIGHT
— VOLUME TWO —

ANN CHRISTOPHER
&
ADRIANNE BYRD

In *Seduced on the Red Carpet*, supermodel Livia Blake is living a glamorous life…but when she meets sexy single father Hunter Chambers, she is tempted with desire and a life that she has never known.

In *Lovers Premiere*, Sofia Wellesley must cope as Limelight Entertainment prepares to merge with their biggest rival. Which means dealing with her worst enemy, Ram Jordan. So why is her traitorous heart clamoring for the man she hates most in the world?

Available now!